Black & White

Black & White

Elizabeth Lee Sorrell

trading as

Yarbrough House Publishing

Trading as Yarbrough House Publishing
For information please email
info@yarbroughhousepublishing.com

www.YarbroughHousePublishing.com

ISBN 978-0-9970132-4-5

First Edition.

Printed in the United States of America

Chapter One

Shantelle is a secretary by title, but in reality she is so much more. She does all the typical secretary jobs. She files. She answers phones. She types. She takes dictation. She keeps up with the books. She keeps up with appointments. She even makes coffee runs. In addition she also keeps local P.D. (police department) out of the way as well as state authorities. She feeds cover stories to the FBI and other government officials. She keeps track of a wide variety of agents. She knows where all field agents and desk warmers are at all times. If any agent goes AWOL at any time, Shantelle is the first to know about it. Each agent checks in with her both before and after an assignment. She takes their statement and fills out the appropriate paperwork. Then she keeps that same paperwork hidden away and locked tight.

Shantelle works for a top secret branch of the CIA. The whole operation is very hush-hush. Neither local, state, nor federal authorities know anything about this top secret branch. Most government officials know nothing at all, and very few CIA know about this branch.

Shantelle's boss, Mr. Hawk, would be lost without her, and he knows it. Mr. Hawk has no organizational skills. He can rarely find a pen without Shantelle's help. That is not to mention how hard a worker Shantelle is. She is focused. She is super efficient, and she does everything that is asked of her and then some. She is the quiet type; she is no nonsense. She never really gets to know anyone.

Jayson has worked for this branch for over five years now. He was chosen for this position for several reasons. He is an outstanding field agent. He thinks quick on his feet. He easily makes executive decisions. He is a natural born leader. He juggles his schedule well. He is also a very laid back man; he does not get into a panic. Unfortunately punctuality is not necessarily a high priority with Jayson.

"You're late," Shantelle said as Jayson walked up to her desk.

"Better late than never," Jayson commented. "They practically begged me to join their executive board. What are they going to do, have the entire meeting without me?"

"Don't underestimate Hawk," Shantelle warned.

"He's mad, huh?" Jayson inquired.

"Mad is not the word," Shantelle answered. "I need to see you as soon as the meeting is over. I need your statement."

"You look busy," Jayson said. Shantelle glanced up at Jayson without a word then promptly returned to her work. "Right, I'm late; we'll talk later," Jayson responded and made his way down the hall to the meeting.

Hawk was still steamed when he came out of the meeting. He started this branch himself fourteen years ago. He takes his job very serious. His job is his life, and he expects everyone involved to take their job serious, especially members of the executive board of directors. Jayson's laid back attitude drives Hawk up the wall, and he cannot stand the way Jayson shows up late for everything.

"Shantelle, these need to be typed up," Hawk said handing her a large stack of papers. "Those notices we talked about last week will need to be mailed out."

"Freeze, Black," Shantelle interrupted.

"Do you have eyes in the back of your head?" Jayson asked.

"Wait right there. I still need your statement. I'll call down and have security stop you if you try to leave," Shantelle warned.

"I wouldn't dream of skipping out on our titillating interview," Jayson said with obvious sarcasm.

Hawk rolled his eyes and continued on with his instructions for Shantelle. "When you get a chance come see me. I have a list of names I need a background on. If I like what I see, I'm going to need some contact information."

Hawk turned and walked into his office. Shantelle turned around to her desk and set the stack of papers down. "Have a seat," she instructed Jayson.

"Is that a secure area?" Jayson joked.

"Drop the smart comments, Black. I don't have time for them," Shantelle said.

"You never have the time. I don't think I've ever seen you take the time to even smile," Jayson returned.

"Stick to the assignment," Shantelle instructed with aggravation.

"Yeah, did you hand pick that assignment for me? It was an open and shut case."

"You had a meeting to get back for," Shantelle replied.

"Come on. It was too easy. I like a challenge," Jayson complained.

"Just tell me what happened."

"The guy was predictable. He was at the precise location you gave me. He had not changed anything about his routine. He had not changed anything about his looks. I arrived Wednesday morning. I had found him by Wednesday night. I had him positively ID'ed and in my sights by Thursday morning. I shot him. He's gone. It's over. I was home by Friday morning."

"You were home yesterday morning," Shantelle responded. "Why are you only now checking in?"

"I had to come in today for the meeting anyway. Why come in two days in a row?" Jayson questioned.

"I need to know exactly when you get back from now on. Hold on while I get your next assignment."

"Wouldn't it be easier if you tagged me with a tracking device? You could attach it to my underwear maybe, won't be going far without those." Jayson asked as Shantelle pulled up assignments on the computer.

"What makes you so sure I don't already have one?" Shantelle asked.

"Was that a joke? Do you have an actual sense of humor? You know, I bet when you leave here at night, you are the sweetest girl that any person has ever met."

"Your assignment is printing out now. I hope it is challenging enough," Shantelle said with a sly smile.

Elizabeth Lee Sorrell

Chapter Two

Jayson did not come back in for almost a month.

"Jayson Black reporting in. My plane got in one hour ago," he said slapping Shantelle's desk.

Shantelle glanced up. "You look jet lagged. What took so long?"

"Oh, ha, ha," Jayson reacted.

"You did say you wanted a challenge. Have a seat," Shantelle said.

Jayson sat down. "I hope you have plenty of time."

"It's my job to listen to your reports and fill out forms. Go."

"You do have a sense of humor. Tell me one thing before we get started. Did you really hand pick that assignment?" Jayson asked with fascination.

"It was one of the hardest cases we had. You wanted a challenge, so I figured you might as well take a crack at it," Shantelle admitted.

"Wow," Jayson mumbled shaking his head. "Okay, so I get there, to the location you gave me, right, and this guy is absolutely nowhere to be found. I looked everywhere. I asked everyone. No one has ever seen this guy. There was no sign that this guy was ever there. I'm just walking around clueless for three days. Then I saw it.

"It was hanging there staring me in the face the whole time. In a little pizza place, there was a small bulletin board with little odds and ends from patrons hanging on it. It was sort of hidden, but there was his name in clear print. It was a hand written note, girl's handwriting. It was a bunch of mushy, gushy stuff basically wishing him luck in Australia.

"This was it. The guy was on the move, and so was I. Now I knew what country, but I had no idea where in Australia. Australia is a large enough country. I was talking with a stewardess on the flight over. She was preoccupied with her cosmetology classes. I showed her the picture. She recognized him, but he looked very different with dark hair. She talked about how the blonde really didn't suit him. After an excruciatingly long discussion about hair color, I finally got out of her that he has dark hair now with blonde highlights. He remembered to dye his eyebrows, and he had a dark goatee. Just before his flight landed the stewardess overheard him on the phone with some doctor. She said that it sounded like he was planning some sort of plastic surgery. She thought the doctor's name was Dr. Grey or something like that.

"It's not much to go on, but it's something. It took me another couple days to find this doctor. He wasn't a very reputable doctor to say the least. It took a little coercing, but I finally got the desired information out of him. Of course, afterwards he did have to find an actual doctor with real medical training. Anyway, there was nowhere for our guy to hide after the hack job that this so called Dr. Grey did on him, but I still can't get near him.

"He keeps eluding me. I kept catching glimpses of him, but that was as close as I can get. This guy was good. I spent another week trying everything I could think of. None of it worked. I was out of ideas, so I called him."

"You what?" Shantelle interrupted.

"Did you have any better ideas?" Jayson asked.

"You just called the guy up as yourself?" Shantelle asked.

"Yeah what was I supposed to do? He knew who I was. I knew who he was, so I called him to set up a meeting. I figured it was the only chance I had left at getting this guy. I called him. He agreed. We met to fight it out once and for all. We set our guns aside to fight hand to hand.

"As it started out we were pretty evenly matched. This guy was good. It was like he could anticipate my every move. He blocked everything I threw at him, and he kept giving it back to me."

By this time Shantelle was propped up on her elbow intently listening to Jayson's encounter. This was more interesting than his normal report, and it was getting more interesting by the minute.

"Now I was at a real loss. We were going to be locked in this endless battle until one of us tired out. We were so evenly matched that there was no way to know which one of us would tire out first. I was beginning to wonder if it would ever end. Then I felt something sharp slide across my side. He had pulled out a knife. He had a knife. I didn't have anything. I only brought one weapon with me, and I had already set it aside like an idiot... Shouldn't you be putting this into the computer or something?"

"I'm getting it. Keep going," Shantelle encouraged eager to hear the rest.

"Okay, if you say so. Anyway, where was I?"

"The other guy had a knife," Shantelle reminded.

"Oh, yeah. So, I'm busy dodging a knife. I've got to get that knife or at least knock it away from him. He had a death grip on that knife and knew how to use it. I was helpless. It was becoming obvious who was going to give out first. I had to do something, but I didn't know what. We had agreed to a straight up hand to hand combat. He broke that agreement, surprise, surprise. All bets were off at this point. I had to do something. I did something I'm not proud of... I saw an opening and I took it. He left himself wide open. I had to do something... I kicked him."

"You kicked him," Shantelle repeated expressionlessly. He couldn't possibly be serious. All this build up, and he kicked him? That was it?

Jayson's eyes widened slightly. He gave Shantelle a funny look and said, "Yeah, I kicked him... between the legs."

Shantelle started to laugh. She couldn't help it. This was absolutely the best report she had ever been given.

Jayson continued on as if he did not notice Shantelle's laughter. "He fell to the ground holding himself. I kicked the knife away and screamed at him to get up. Of course, he didn't. I grabbed my gun and screamed for him to get up again. He was lying on the ground crying, and I shot him."

Shantelle was still laughing.

"Would you please stop? There's nothing funny about this. You don't do that. You don't kick a guy there. That was a low blow on my part."

"Oh, please, like bringing a knife was any better. That guy was a terrorist. The last thing you need to be worried about now is kicking him between the legs," Shantelle said.

"Anyway, I went back to the hotel after that. I got cleaned up, bandaged my side, and headed for the airport," Jayson finished.

"You haven't seen a doctor yet about your side? How bad is it?" Shantelle asked very seriously.

Jayson stood up. He turned and lifted his shirt above the bandage. The bandage itself was at least a foot long. Blood had soaked through the bandage.

"It's still bleeding," Shantelle said.

"It was. I think it's stopped now," Jayson responded.

"I'm setting you up an appointment with the doctor right now," Shantelle said.

"Listen, I'm going to take a couple days before I pick up my next assignment," Jayson said.

Shantelle looked up at him like he was stupid. "You're not getting another assignment for at least a week."

"I'll be fine in a couple days," Jayson told her.

"You will take at least a week, maybe more depending on what the doctor says," Shantelle insisted.

"You're serious, aren't you?" Jayson asked.

"It's for your own good," Shantelle said.

"Well, I guess if you have my best interests in mind, how could I refuse?" Jayson asked with a smile.

"You can't refuse. I'm in charge of passing out assignments," Shantelle reminded him.

"You know you're pretty tough for someone so sweet. How does someone so sweet end up in a place like this anyway? You just don't seem to me that you have the personality for this line of work. How did you get introduced to this?"

"I was born into it," Shantelle answered shortly.

"How are you born into a job? Is there some CIA royalty that I don't know about?" Jayson returned.

"My parents were both spies. I never went to school. I was home schooled. I played with other home schooled kids whose parents were also spies. This is the only world I've ever known," Shantelle explained.

"Wow, so how long have you been with this branch?"

"It's been about fourteen and a half years."

"With this particular branch?" Jayson questioned.

"Yes, I started with Hawk when I was eighteen."

"So you've been here from the ground up? You helped start this branch."

"This branch is Hawks baby. I just help out here and there, wherever I can," Shantelle said.

"No wonder you know the ins and outs of this place like nobody else," Jayson contemplated.

"Okay, well, the doctor will be waiting. You better get a move on," Shantelle suggested.

Chapter Three

Jayson Black showed up again exactly one week later. "Okay, I'm ready to go," he said.

"What did the doctor say?" Shantelle questioned.

"He wanted to staple my side, but I just wasn't going for that," Jayson said shaking his head. "The recovery time is too long."

"What did he do?" Shantelle asked.

"Stitches," Jayson replied quickly.

"How many?"

"Too many. They come out tomorrow morning."

"You still have stitches?" Shantelle pushed.

"Yeah, but they come out tomorrow."

"You're not getting another assignment yet."

"It's really not that big a deal. I'll get them taken out tomorrow on my way out. Everything will be fine," Jayson argued.

"Oh, yeah, everything will be fine as you rip open your side. How about I give the doctor a call real quick to check in?" Shantelle countered.

"How about we just do things your way? There's not much use arguing with you. I imagine that you've heard every argument imaginable anyway," Jayson gave in.

"No, actually, you are the only one who argues with me," Shantelle added.

"You're kidding. Okay, fine, have it your way. When can I come back?" Jayson relented. He was giving in way to easily; now Shantelle knew that he didn't have clearance from the doctor. It aggravated Shantelle that Jayson really believed she was that stupid.

"We'll talk in a week," Shantelle said.

"A week!" Jayson reacted. "I'm ready now!"

"We'll talk in one week," Shantelle repeated.

Jayson started to speak but stopped himself. He slapped the desk top in anger instead and just left.

Jayson came back one week later with a whole new attitude. He walked over to Shantelle's desk. He lifted his shirt and twirled around. "Do I meet approval?"

"What did the doctor say?" Shantelle asked.

"I don't care what the doctor said. I asked if I met your approval. He gave me the okay days ago. Do you know that when I left here last week, not two hours later I ripped apart half the stitches?"

"The doctor said you were okay?" Shantelle questioned. "Do I need to call Dr. Hanson myself?"

"Be my guest," Jayson offered. "I have his okay."

"That's great, but it doesn't matter. You have a meeting in three days," Shantelle reminded him.

"Come on. Have a heart. I've been off work for two weeks. I'm ready to go back to work. Don't you have one easy case, something I can do in a couple days?" Jayson pleaded. "I'm going stir crazy."

"There is one guy who has been reported back in the states," Shantelle offered.

"Here in the states? Doesn't that make him homeland security's problem?" Jayson questioned.

"Do you want the assignment or not?" "I don't want to overstep my boundaries. Are you sure the case is cool?"

"It's still our case, so I guess it is cool. Look, if you don't want the case, I'll give it to someone else."

"No, I'll take it," Jayson replied.

Shantelle pulled up the case file on her computer and printed it. She stood up and walked around the desk to get the information out of the printer.

Jayson let out a wolf whistle. "What are you so dressed up for?"

Her outfit wasn't anything great. It was classic work apparel, but it was nice to be appreciated now and then. The guys around here didn't ever notice, and she had no life outside work. "I've got to attend a grant meeting this afternoon," Shantelle answered.

"A grant for a top secret organization?" Jayson inquired.

"You have to word things just right. Use a lot of fancy words. No one ever understands exactly what the organization is, what it does, or what the money is used for," Shantelle explained.

"So money is getting pretty tight around here?"
"You're on the board," Shantelle reminded him.

"Yeah, I know. I thought that was why I was put on the board, to help out with the financial aspect. I don't know why they don't let me take a look at the books."

Hawk cleared his throat from his office doorway. "Shantelle, get Mr. Black a copy of whatever he needs. I need those papers I asked you for this morning."

"They're on the corner of my desk," Shantelle answered. Hawk took the large stack of papers and went back into his office.

"I'm sorry. I didn't mean to put more work on you," Jayson apologized.

"It's no problem. It's really not as hard as it sounds. Do you want a copy of everything or just the financial aspects?" Shantelle asked.

"Spare me. I only want the financial aspects."

"Do you still want the assignment?"

"Let me take a look at it." Jayson took the assignment from Shantelle and read over it real quick. "Yeah, I can get both done before the meeting."

"Are you sure?" Shantelle double checked.

"Sure. This case is easy enough, and I'm a wiz at finances believe it or not," Jayson replied.

Shantelle sat down at her computer and started pulling up information. "How far back do you want me to go?"

"Oh, I don't know. You have your hand in everything that goes on around here. How long would you say there has been a problem?" Jayson inquired.

"It came on slow."

"Do you think five years would go back far enough?"

"Why not?" Shantelle responded. She clicked print on the computer. "Okay, it's printing. It's a lot of information, so it may take a while."

"That's it?" Jayson asked with surprise. Jayson thought that it was going to take a while to find information from that long ago.

"That's it when you know what you are doing."

"That's perfect. You know that this whole department would be lost without you. Hey, Shantelle, you said your parents are spies. Do they work for this branch?" Jayson asked.

"I said they were spies. My parents are dead," Shantelle replied.

"Oh, I'm sorry," Jayson reacted. He was such an idiot, bringing up a painful past.

"Why? You aren't the one who killed them," Shantelle said.

"They were murdered?"

"They were spies," Shantelle said as if all spies died as a result of murder.

"Not all spies die that way," Jayson rebuked.

"You can get your information out of the printer. I've got to get everything together for the grant meeting," Shantelle said ignoring Jayson's comment.

Jayson waited for the printer to finish. He took the information and started off.

"Don't be late," Shantelle called after him.

"That doesn't sound a thing like me," Jayson laughed. He didn't stick around to see if Shantelle cracked a smile, but he was willing to bet money that she didn't. That girl was seriously uptight.

Chapter Four

Despite Shantelle's warning, Jayson was late for the meeting. "You're late," she accused again. It seemed like she was constantly warning him not to be late or telling him he was late.

Jayson had a serious look on his face. "These books are a joke," he said holding up the financial information that he had gotten from Shantelle three days ago. "They are so bad that I'm not sure if it was done on purpose or if the person doing them is that clueless. They've made a huge mess of things, but there is a simple answer."

"They've already started," Shantelle told him.

"Okay, thanks," Jayson said as he hurried down the hall.

They had already started without Jayson. That wasn't a big surprise, but just how far they had gotten without him came as a shock. The board was in the middle of going over new financial policies when Jayson walked in.

"Black, you're late," Hawk barked.

It turned out that Jayson had missed the vote on a financial solution. The board gave Jayson a brief overview of the new policies.

Jayson had been in the meeting for a while before the screaming started. Once the screaming started, it could be heard down the hall all the way to Shantelle's desk.

"You are jackasses if you think anyone is going to agree to that," Jayson's voice carried.

"You should have been here on time and maybe you could have put in your two cents," another man returned loudly.

"Now, boys," Hawk intervened.

The hall got quiet again for a few seconds. Then Jayson's voice roared again. "Don and Robin are jackasses. No one else is that stupid. Why do ya'll choose the stupidest solution you can find when there is an easy solution?"

"If you found an easy solution, you should have been here on time to present your ideas," the other man came back.

"Oh, get off it, Perkins!" Jayson yelled.

The room got quiet again, and only seconds later the men began filing out. The first four men walked down the hallway without a word. They moved past Shantelle's desk without acknowledgment and left immediately.

Next Hawk came down the hallway followed by Jayson. Hawk stopped at Shantelle's desk, so Jayson did also. "Shantelle, I need to talk with you," Hawk said. "Black, if you don't mind. . ."

"Oh, no, not at all," Jayson returned. "Go right ahead. I'll give my report when you finish."

"Black," Hawk said authoritatively.

"I'm on the board. Am I not?" Jayson asked.

"Yes," Hawk answered.

"I've been left out of every decision so far and every vote. I have no intention of leaving your side, Hawk. So, you go right ahead and have your little talk," Jayson told.

"Black, be reasonable," Hawk negotiated.

"If you can tell me that as a board member I don't have the right to be here, then I'll leave," Jayson offered.

Hawk sighed disappointedly. "Shantelle, have a seat. This won't be easy. This is the hardest thing I've had to do since starting this department. You know the books better than anyone. You know the struggle that we've hit around here lately. It's the board's decision to let you go," he said solemnly.

Shantelle sat and stared at Hawk in shock. Hawk wasn't one to joke much, especially when it came to work, but this had to be a joke. Didn't it?

"Whoa, let go?" Jayson reacted. "What happened to the salary cut?"

"As a secretary, it was felt that Shantelle was expendable. It is the board's belief that we can serve as our own secretary and that agents can enter their own reports to the computer," Hawk tried to explain.

"That's insane! Do you have any idea how much she does around here?" Jayson questioned.

"I do, but I set the board up so that no man could acquire too much power, no man including myself. I was simply out voted. There was nothing left to do. Even with your vote, it would not have been enough. She has two weeks from today. I'm sorry, Shantelle," Hawk apologized and disappeared into his office. It didn't change anything, but Hawk did look truly upset.

Jayson plopped down into a chair. "This is unreal," he complained. "There is such a simple solution. Why do they have to go and complicate things with the most off the wall ideas they can dream up. Have you heard their so called proposal?" Shantelle did not respond. She couldn't find her voice. "Now keep in mind that they actually voted to go with this. They are requiring all single agents to marry so that they can afford to have their salary reduced. They aren't just requiring every single person to marry, but they are encouraged to marry someone from this department. We just found out they're letting you go. All this is supposed to reduce payroll, but their problem isn't in payroll. I don't understand their reasoning even if the problem was in payroll. They think that having dual incomes will somehow enable people to get by on less individually. I don't know, unless they are thinking that one house note and one set of utility bills will make that big a difference. That's why they're pushing so hard to get people to marry in house; otherwise, it wouldn't help a thing. The agent still might not be able to make ends meet on a dual salary with the cuts they want to make."

"I don't know what you're complaining about," Shantelle spoke up for the first time. Her shock had been replaced by rage. "At least you still have a job. While you're complaining about a salary reduction, y'all already get paid well; you could easily make it even with a salary reduction. I was barely squeaking by as it was. This is the only job I've ever had. This is all I know how to do, and this country is in the middle of an economic recession. What am I supposed to do? Where will I go?"

Jayson did not know the answer. They sat in complete silence for several minutes while they both thought over the situation.

Finally Jayson sat straight up in the chair. "I've got it! Let's get married."

"What!?" Shantelle reacted. It was official; he was insane.

"I know I sound as crazy as them, but it is the perfect revenge. Imagine it. I am now required to marry someone else in this department to keep my job. You have two weeks left. You are still a part of this department. As long as we do it before your two weeks are over, I'm following orders, and you won't have to worry about money. I make more than enough to take care of both of us. Even with a salary reduction there will be enough to get by. No offence, but I've seen what you make; it couldn't get any worse," Jayson said.

"Don't you have a report to give me?" Shantelle asked trying to change the subject.

"Just think about it for a couple days and get back to me," Jayson said.

"Your report," Shantelle pushed.

"Yeah, okay," Jayson agreed but did not start.

"Go," Shantelle instructed.

The last two board members made their way down the hall. As they walked past Shantelle's desk, one man said, "Tough break, Shelly. Better luck next time." The self important jerk still didn't even know her name, but he sure made it a point to stop and rub it in that she was out on her butt.

Shantelle glared at the men and watched them into the elevator. Her rage escalated with every step they took. "I'm in," she told Jayson. "Your report, Go."

Jayson smiled slyly and started with his report. "It was a simple open and shut case. He was back in the states to see about his mother who is in the hospital. He was easy to find, easy to track, and easy to kill. He was staying in a hotel two blocks away from the hospital. I used a silencer and put a bullet into his head. Problem solved."

Shantelle did not say anything for another minute. "What was the room number?" she asked.

"Is that important?" Jayson wondered.

"Yes."

"It was one-o-six. You've never asked for those sort of details before," Jayson pointed out.

"It was never on home turf before. Clean up has always been someone else's problem in times past. Are you sure no one saw you?"

"I'm one hundred percent positive. This wasn't my first assignment," Jayson replied.

"Okay, great… What am I supposed to do now?" Shantelle mumbled. Her rage had turned to hopeless-ness. Was this grief? Her emotions were all over the place.

"I have no idea. I've never been on your end of things," Jayson admitted.

"What?" Jayson threw Shantelle for a minute. She had forgotten that he was there. "Oh, it isn't that. I know what to do about the case. Forget about it. I was talking to myself."

"Are you going to be okay?" Jayson checked.

"Yeah, I'll be fine. Everything is still sinking in. I don't know what to do without work," Shantelle replied.

"If you're worried about money, don't. I told you I make enough, and I'm excellent with finances."

"It's not even that. I'm not the type person who can do nothing, and now I have nothing to do," Shantelle explained.

Jayson nodded thoughtfully. "Maybe you could do volunteer work somewhere."

Shantelle looked at Jayson like that was the stupidest thing he could have said. "Where would I go to volunteer? What could I do? I'm no good to anyone except CIA."

"I'm sure that's not true... Maybe you could volunteer up here. You already have the clearance. Everyone knows and trusts you, and goodness knows that we could use the help with you gone. I'm sure that Hawk will be lost without you. I've never had to enter my own report onto the computer. I wouldn't know how, and I can't be the only one." Jayson watched Shantelle. She was focused, thinking about what he had just said. "This whole thing would be picture perfect revenge. You still coming up to help would be even sweeter."

"How would that be revenge? I would be coming up here and still doing all the work for them for free," Shantelle challenged.

"Exactly! These are some very proud men. They are under the impression that they don't need you. They believe that the work will still get done without you around. We both know that's not true. When you are still coming up, still doing the work, that's the only way things are getting done, and they are still depending on you. It would be proof positive that they cannot function without you. They cannot run this place without you. They simply could not do it without you. That would be like a kick in the pants to such proud men."

Shantelle did not say anything. Jayson was not sure if she understood his point of view; he was not sure if she had even heard him. That was when he realized that he had not thought much about her point of view either. Weren't most women always dreaming about Mr. Right and forever? Maybe she was holding out for something more.

Jayson laid a hand on Shantelle's shoulder to be sure he had her attention. "Maybe you should give it a few days to think this over before you make a decision. I mean, it's easier for me. I'm not looking for more. My job is my life, and I'm satisfied with that."

"Nope, I've made my decision. I'm in. When do want to do this?" Shantelle insisted.

"Are you sure you shouldn't take a little more time?"

"Absolutely. You said the job is your life. You chose that. The job is my life too, but it chose me. This is all I have, and I've never looked for more. It never occurred that there was anything else out there for me. When do you want to do this?" Shantelle asked again.

"Wow, you need to get a life. How about this weekend?" Jayson suggested.

"That's fine," Shantelle agreed.

"Okay, I'll meet you Saturday, ten o'clock at the court-house," Jayson planned.

"Got it. I'll see you there."

Chapter Five

"You're late," Shantelle accused when Jayson got to the courthouse Saturday.

"I'd think you'd be used to it by now," Jayson defended. "I'm almost surprised to see you. I halfway didn't expect you to show up."

"What's that supposed to mean?" Shantelle reacted.

"Nothing. It's just that I wouldn't blame you if you didn't want to go through with this. That's all. You have a lot to lose."

"I have a lot to lose either road I take. At least on this road the decision is mine and I get to tick off a few board members on my way out."

"It's kind of funny to see this side of you. I never pictured you as the type to fight authority," Jayson commented.

"I'm not under normal circumstances, but this particular board is not much of an authority."

"I've got to agree with you on that point. What I don't understand is why Hawk doesn't fight back harder. They are running his department into the ground. Well, anyway, if you're ready we can go ahead and get this over with."

"Get this over with," Shantelle repeated on a sigh. "Just what every girl longs to hear. Oh well, that's more than I would have ever heard on the path I was headed down. You're sure that this is going to get under the board members' skin?"

"Absolutely."

"Okay. Let's do this."

"Are you sure you can handle this?" Jayson asked nervously.

"I can do this. Can you?" Shantelle shot back.

"Okay, it's this way," Jayson said and walked into the building. Shantelle followed and they started down a long quiet hall. "Hey, Shantelle, what is your last name? I never caught it," Jayson asked quietly.

"White," Shantelle answered.

"Black and White, what a pair," Jayson laughed.

The judge was an older man; he was easily in his late sixties or even early seventies. He was not too far from his retirement. He had a large, toothy grin and he smiled constantly. He had a loud deep laugh. He was caring and very friendly.

"Well, well, what a lovely couple! Ya'll look beautiful together. It's been a long time since I've had such an attractive couple in here. Are we waiting on family and friends?" the judge asked with a smile.

"No, sir, it's just us," Jayson answered.

"Oh, there is no one here to share this special day? Well, that's okay. The important thing is that the two of you are in love and getting married. Love is such a wonderful institute when it is done for the right reasons. Marriage should never be entered into lightly. It is a very serious matter. Don't you agree?" the judge asked.

"Oh, yes, sir, it is an extremely serious matter. It is a precious union," Jayson agreed.

"Yes, it is. It is so precious. So, how long have ya'll known each other?" the judge asked.

"Just over five years," Jayson replied.

"My, my, it can't be said that ya'll rushed into anything. How did you meet?" the judge asked.

"We work together, or at least we did until recently. Shantelle was a secretary at the office I work at, but we were forced to let her go due to cutbacks," Jayson explained. It was always best to stick to as much truth as possible. It made your cover story easier to remember that way.

"Oh, how dreadful! I'm so sorry to hear that," the judge consoled.

"Don't worry about us. We are going to be just fine," Jayson smiled.

"Ah, young love. I remember those days well, when nothing can hurt you as long as you have each other. Take my advice. Hold on to these days for as long as you can and cherish them."

"Of course, your honor," Jayson responded.

The judge laughed. Then he turned to Shantelle. "You are quiet."

"She's shy. I guess that's why we didn't rush into anything," Jayson joked.

The judge laughed and said, "There's nothing wrong with that. I was shy once myself if you can believe that."

The wedding ceremony took longer than anticipated because the judge talked so much.

"He knows," Shantelle mumbled as she and Jayson made their way outside.

"Knows what?" Jayson asked.

"He knows what we're up to," Shantelle clarified.

"How could a county judge possibly know what's going on in a secret department of the CIA? He doesn't know anything."

"Why was he asking all those questions and talking about getting married for the right reasons? He knows we weren't being honest," Shantelle protested.

"He is a friendly old man who screens everyone who comes through his chambers. He probably questions everyone. I mean I've had to tell some whoppers throughout the course of my career, but that really was one of the more simple ones to sell. He wanted it to be true. From the moment we walked in, he thought we looked good together, and he wanted to believe us," Jayson explained.

"So, now what?"

"Well, I'm going to the office Monday morning to pick up my next assignment. I guess I'll see you there," Jayson replied.

"Okay, see you then," Shantelle responded, and they both left.

Elizabeth Lee Sorrell

Chapter Six

Shantelle and Jayson arrived at the office at basically the same time Monday morning. They met at the door. "What are you doing here so early?" Shantelle asked.

"Well, you know what they say," Jayson laughed.

"No, what do they say?"

"The early bird gets the worm," Jayson recited.

There were two guards waiting in the lobby. "Good morning, Shantelle," they greeted.

"Good morning," Shantelle returned.

The guards tipped their heads at Jayson, and the four of them climbed into the elevator. There were three more guards waiting on the third floor.

The three guards from the third floor were all sitting together just outside the elevator. When the elevator opened, they stood up and started stretching.

"Good morning, boys," Shantelle greeted. She, Jayson, and the first two guards stepped off the elevator.

"Good night," the second set of guards said as they stepped into the elevator.

Shantelle walked to her desk and started setting things out for the day, and the two guards started making their rounds. Shantelle waited for the two guards to get out of sight; then she asked Jayson, "What worm are you trying to catch?"

"Someone will have to break it to Hawk about this weekend," Jayson replied with an all too eager smirk.

"I would kind of like to tell Hawk myself if you don't mind." It would come better from her, not that it would go over well from either one of them, but she did owe it to him to tell Hawk herself.

"No problem. If you want to, you can have at it. It won't hurt my feelings one little bit," Jayson admitted. "Are you always the first one here?"

"Yeah, you've still got a while before Hawk gets here," Shantelle answered.

Jayson took a seat in front of Shantelle's desk. "Wow, this place is really empty. How long will it be until someone else gets here?"

Shantelle kept working. "In about thirty minutes, people will start slowly trickling in."

Shantelle was right on it. About thirty minutes later, almost to the minute, people started to come in one by one. They each one greeted Shantelle by name. They looked at Jayson, but no one spoke.

Jayson did not know many of the people who he worked with. The only times he came into the office were for a board meeting or to report in and pick up the next assignment.

"I did not realize how many people were involved in this department until I started going over the books," Jayson commented to Shantelle.

"Everyone you've seen this morning is technical staff. Most of them have already been given their pink slips."

"That is insane."

"The handful of technical staff left have past experience as field agents. They are a double threat. They don't get paid much more than me. They all came off the field for their own personal reasons, but they would all gladly take on an assignment if asked. They're being used, and they don't even realize it." Shantelle told him with venom.

"That's terrible. Are there not enough field agents to cover the work load?" Jayson asked.

"Right now there is a decent ratio. You don't see as many field agents, because they are like you. They only come in to pick up assignments or give a report. Right now there is a steady flow that works well, but I don't expect that to last much longer," Shantelle answered.

"Why is that?"

"I don't know if the other board members went over the books as well as you did or not, but you can't learn everything you need to know from those books. You are far from the only single field agent. In fact, most of the men and women out there on assignment are single. You may have the most unique protest, but you are not the only one who will have a problem with the new policies. As a matter of fact, there are several who are in a serious relationship with someone who is not in the CIA. I'm sure that they would rather quit than marry someone else. There are several who I can see quitting just to make a point, and of course, there is always that group who will not follow a new policy until they are forced into it," Shantelle explained.

"That's very interesting. So, you know the field agents around here pretty well," Jayson noticed.

"I don't have much of a choice. You get to know someone whether you want to or not when you are taking reports."

"Really? I don't feel like we know each other at all."

"I said I got to know ya'll. I never said ya'll got to know me. To be honest you probably know more about me than the others, and that's because you ask ten zillion personal questions," Shantelle corrected.

"No one said you had to answer. You could have told me to stop asking anytime you were ready… This ought to be interesting. Tell me about myself," Jayson requested.

"You're outgoing. There is not a shy bone in your body. You take the cautious approach when possible, but you don't shy away from the more risky approaches when necessary. You think things through and take the path of the most logical plan. You are determined; you will do whatever it takes to finish a task. You are good; you have every right to brag, but don't. You could easily get an inflated head, but you keep your ego in check for the most part."

"That's not all there is to me. You know my work habits. You don't know me," Jayson retorted.

"You talk too much. You ask too many questions. You think you're sly. You work too much."

"Okay, okay, isn't there anything positive?" Jayson interrupted.

"You are well mannered," Shantelle admitted.

"Well, that's something I guess. Is that it?" Jayson pushed.

"You're living a dream. You've wanted to be a CIA agent since you were a kid…"

The elevator door opened and out stepped Hawk, Perkins, and one other board member.

"What are ya'll doing here?" Jayson reacted.

"What are you doing here so early?" Hawk returned.

"I'm here to pick up an assignment."

Perkins walked over to the desk. He looked down on Jayson. "We're here to make sure that the new policies are enforced correctly and with sternness," he said with a beat that attitude.

"I met up with them on my way in," Hawk added. "I was just explaining that I am fully capable of handling things on this end."

Perkins ignored Hawk without ever taking his eyes off Jayson. "Have you given any thought to the new policies?" he asked Jayson.

"I sure have," Jayson replied.

"Have you decided yet to comply?"

"I have actually."

"Good. Have you given any thought to who you will join forces with?" Perkins asked.

"As a matter of fact, I've given that a lot of thought, and I went ahead and took care of that this weekend."

Shantelle cleared her throat trying to get Jayson's attention, but it was no use. Jayson and Perkins were intensely focused on each other. He was going to open his big mouth and stick his even bigger foot in it, and who was going to pay the price? Shantelle.

"You've already gotten married?" Perkins questioned skeptically.

"That's what I said," Jayson responded.

"And who would that be so that I can go ahead and put that in my records?" Perkins inquired. The smug triumph was easily audible in his voice.

"I think you've already had the pleasure of meeting Shantelle," Jayson blurted without thought. Right in front of Hawk.

Perkins jerked his attention to Hawk. Hawk turned his attention to Shantelle. Shantelle stared back at Hawk. Now what was she supposed to say. She should have told him herself. She could see the hurt in his eyes even if no one else in the room knew what to look for.

Perkins turned back to Jayson. "Do you mean Ms. White?"

"Not anymore. I mean Mrs. Black," Jayson corrected with a superior attitude.

Perkins grinned down at Jayson. "You always think that you know best. You think that you have to prove a point, but this time you have backed yourself into a corner. You haven't read over the new policies yet, have you? Let me try to explain. You were required to marry. You were encouraged, and let me be perfectly clear on this point. You were encouraged to marry another field agent. That was to look out for you. Ms. White was let go to reduce payroll. All field agents' salary will be cut in half. Our thinking was that together you would make the equivalent of one current salary which would be sufficient enough." Perkins turned to Hawk and asked, "Did you know about this?"

"I want to see the two of you in my office now," Hawk barked.

Shantelle and Jayson followed Hawk into the office.

"What is going on around here?" Hawk asked.

Neither Shantelle nor Jayson appeared to hear Hawk.

"Half?" Shantelle demanded her eyes boring into Jayson. Perkins's words were still echoing through her head. That was a significant cut. No, that wasn't just significant; it was huge.

"Come on. Do you honestly think I knew that? This is the first I've heard of that. I never dreamed that they would cut it by that much," Jayson shot back.

"Shantelle?" Hawk almost shouted.

"I wanted to talk to you first, but big mouth over there has no self control," Shantelle responded.

"We can do this. Everything will be fine. I can figure this out," Jayson mumbled to himself. "Hawk, I need some paper, two pencils, and a calculator."

Hawk handed Jayson the paper, pencils, and calculator he asked for. Jayson slid a paper and pencil toward Shantelle. "Write down all your current expenses."

"Now, look. I don't like these so called polices any more than the two of you do. I have every intention of fighting this to the very end, but your smart-aleck antics are not helping." Shantelle handed the paper back to Jayson who started adding things together on the calculator. Hawk continued talking. "The best thing that you can do right now is to go back out there and tell Perkins that this whole thing was a misguided hoax."

"Can't," Jayson broke in.

"Can't?" Hawk repeated. "Black, I don't think you understand. This is not a request. This is an order. Get out there and tell him this was a hoax."

"We can't do that," Jayson insisted. "It isn't a joke"

"What are you saying?"

"We really went through with it," Shantelle owned up to. "We went down to the courthouse this weekend, and we got married."

"You did what?!" Hawk hollered. "I can't believe what I'm hearing. Black, this is by far the stupidest thing you have ever pulled, and now you've drug Shantelle down with you. Shantelle, I expect this sort of thing from Black, but I expected better out of you. What has gotten into you? What was going through your head? I am so disappointed."

Shantelle was disappointed in herself also. What a fool she was! It was a rash move that wasn't guaranteed to ruffle the feathers of any of the board members, but she had gone along with it anyway.

"You're not helping. Do you want the whole building to hear you screaming at us? What's done is done. We can only go forward from this point," Jayson said calmly.

"I didn't have a lot of choices left open," Shantelle defended.

"Black is right about one thing. What's done is done. Ya'll made your decision, and now you have to deal with the consequences," Hawk puffed.

Shantelle and Jayson started to leave. "Ah, leave the calculator, Black," Hawk called. "I'm sure Shantelle has one at her desk that you can use."

Shantelle and Jayson left Hawk's office. Perkins was sitting at Shantelle's desk waiting. "If you'll excuse me, Mr. Perkins, I do have a lot of work to do while I still have a job," Shantelle said.

"Oh, of course, excuse me," Perkins said as he stood up letting Shantelle have her chair back. "Is anyone going to explain what's going on? What was all that about? Where's Hawk?"

"He's in his office. He has work to do also," Jayson replied smartly.

"What was the yelling about?" Perkins asked.

"I don't have to answer to you, Perkins. You don't need to know everything that goes on between me and Hawk. What is it that you want?" Jayson returned.

"I've already told you what I want. I want to be proof positive that the new policies are carried out, so did you or didn't you?" Perkins questioned impatiently.

"Oh yeah, we did."

"Well, you've finally done it, haven't you?" Perkins smirked.

"Haven't we already established that a couple times," Jayson responded.

"Now what are you going to do?"

"I'm assuming that you mean financially since you got such a pleasure out of telling me just how much my salary was to be cut. For the record, our personal financial situation is none of your business, but I was actually about to sit down with Shantelle and crunch some numbers. I'm sure we'll be fine. I did have a few questions though; maybe you could help me out. Are the board members taking a pay cut?" Jayson asked.

"Decidedly not."

"I figured as much. Now, let's see. I currently get paid extra for being on the board. So, do I get cut only on the field agent portion of my salary, or do I get cut on the whole thing? Well, it doesn't really matter. The cut can be on the whole; we'll still be fine."

"You're the financial expert. Whatever you think is best, I'm sure it will work out. Now, if you'll both excuse me, I didn't come all the way up here today to sit around and shoot the breeze," Perkins said; then he disappeared down the hall.

"Everything is not going to be fine, is it?" Shantelle asked Jayson.

"I don't know yet," Jayson admitted. "Do you have a calculator?"

Shantelle pulled a calculator out of the top drawer of her desk and handed it to Jayson. Jayson started crunching numbers again, and Shantelle went back to her work.

Chapter Seven

"Oh boy!" Jayson mumbled under his breath.

"What does that mean?" Shantelle questioned feeling none too secure at the moment.

"I've cut everything down to the absolute bare necessities, and we still can't make ends meet. That's with two houses. I know that this isn't what you agreed to, but if we cut out one house, we live comfortably."

"Oh boy," Shantelle repeated Jayson's words from earlier. "What have we done? We can't. We can't. My house is way too small. It would never house two people. It's barely large enough for one."

"My house could easily house two. There is a guest room that is empty. Plus I'm away a lot on assignment anyway. There would be plenty of room, and I wouldn't be in your way all that often," Jayson said.

"This whole thing is a mess. We've got to..." Shantelle was unable to finish her thought.

A field agent walked off the elevator and straight over to Shantelle's desk. He looked winded and red-faced. "What is this all about," he demanded as he slammed a manila folder down on the desk. "This was delivered this morning. Is this a joke?"

"What is that?" Shantelle asked calmly.

"It was labeled new policies," the agent answered.

"Wow, that was fast," Jayson reacted.

Shantelle shot Jayson a stay out of this, look. "I'm afraid this is no joke. The board met last week and voted on new policies."

"Maybe you can explain these so-called new policies. Maybe tell me how they can do this. They can't do this. They can't require that. I will not roll over," he shouted angrily.

"I really don't know much about the new policies. You'll have to talk with Hawk or one of the other board members," Shantelle broke in still remaining calm.

"I want to talk to Hawk," the agent demanded.

"Here comes one of the board members right now. What luck!" Jayson said motioning at Perkins who was coming back up the hall.

The agent stormed up to Perkins and asked, "Are you on the board?"

"Yes," Perkins answered.

"Do you know anything about the new policies?" the agent asked.

"Yes, I do. As a matter of fact, I'm here to make sure they are enforced," Perkins replied.

"Enforced?" the agent reacted his flustered face going beet red. "Enforce this. I will not comply."

"You must comply in order to retain your position," Perkins warned.

Shantelle buzzed Hawk's office. "Agent Kingsley is here. He's asking about the policies."

"Send him in," Hawk responded.

"That's easier said than done. He's already run into Perkins."

Hawk came rushing out of his office, but he was too late. The usually calm Kingsley was not easily agitated. He put up with a lot, but when he blew his top, it was all over. Those were the times he tended to do a little pruning. He would cut ties to people who were difficult, and as far as Shantelle knew he had never second guessed any of those decisions. Perkins was difficult to be sure.

"Retain my position," the agent repeated. "Why don't you do my job? I quit."

"Kingsley, calm down. Let's discuss this with a cool head," Hawk pleaded.

"I'm through discussing. You can keep your new policies," Kingsley said, and he threw his own copy of the new policies at Hawk.

Kingsley marched out without ever slowing up. He did not flinch, and he never looked back. There was no doubt in Shantelle's mind; they had seen the last of Agent Kingsley.

"And the first one bites the dust," Jayson chanted.

"Black, stay out of this," Hawk barked. "You've done enough damage."

"What did I do?" Jayson reacted.

Hawk ignored Jayson. Perkins ignored Jayson. Shantelle seemed to be the only one who heard Jayson, but she had already removed herself from the entire situation. It was safest not to cross an irate and volatile field agent no matter how calm they usually were.

Hawk looked sternly at Perkins and never said a word, but apparently the message indeed got across loud and clear. Perkins began to shift his weight. He started fidgeting nervously. "I know what you're thinking. Don't worry. He's only one man. We don't need him."

Hawk still did not say a word. He stared Perkins down. "How many do you not need?" Jayson butted in.

"Black, I've already told you once to stay out of this. Now, I'm warning you. I am still your boss. There will be repercussions. Do not cross me again," Hawk growled.

Jayson, taking a hint, sat down in front of Shantelle's desk. Shantelle was busy pulling files and trying hard not to be involved.

"Have all the agents received a copy?" Hawk asked Perkins.

"Most of them have. I have a list of names that I need a current address, and I have another list of names that I need to know when they will return home."

"Can I see the list?" Hawk requested.

Perkins pulled a folded piece of paper from his pocket and handed it to Hawk. Hawk unfolded the paper and looked it over. He laid the paper down on Shantelle's desk and said, "Shantelle, can you get on this right away?"

"Yes, sir," she answered. Shantelle sat down at the computer, picked up the list, and got started immediately.

"Perkins, you have no finesse. I would appreciate it from here on out if you would let me talk with the agents. You don't know how to talk with these men; you are a different breed," Hawk negotiated.

"You got that right," Jayson mumbled.

"Black!" Hawk snapped.

"Staying out of it, sir," Jayson back tracked.

"Hawk, I will be around to be sure that everything is done correctly with optimum proficiency," Perkins said.

"That's fine," Hawk agreed. "I'm not asking you to leave. All I'm asking you to do is keep your mouth shut, and let me handle my men."

"It won't hurt anything for you to make the first attempt. I prefer that you do your own dirty work. I'm simply here to make sure you don't make any exceptions for anyone," Perkins replied.

"I don't like what you are insinuating. I know my job, and I know my place. I am strict at times. I am soft at times. I may even be mean at times, but I am always fair. I treat all my men the same. I suggest you do the same," Hawk lectured.

"What does that mean?" Perkins challenged.

"I've got that information you wanted," Shantelle interrupted. She pulled the papers off the printer, straightened them up, and handed them to Perkins.

"Thank you, Shantelle," Hawk said. He was obviously grateful for the interruption.

"That was fast," Perkins commented. "It's a shame that we could not afford to keep you. You are proficient. I'm going to take this information with me and go get started."

"Why don't you do that?" Jayson added with potent irritation.

"Black, I said shut up," Hawk shouted. Perkins got in the elevator and left. Hawk turned back to Jayson. "Why are you still here?"

"I'm here to pick up my new assignment."

"I wish you would do it and get out of my hair."

"I was just about to," Jayson assured him. "Why do you let him do that? You let him run the show. It's all yes, sir. Whatever you say, sir. You just laid down and played dead. Have you tried to fight this at all? Have you ever stood up to him? He is running your agents off. Does that mean anything to you? What about Shantelle? She works hard everyday for this department. He comes in here and treats her like she is dirt beneath his fingernails. She does not deserve that."

"Do you think I don't know that?" Hawk shot back. "She doesn't deserve the way he treats her, and she doesn't deserve to lose her job. She works harder than anyone else up here. She knows better than anyone how this department is run, and everyone knows that. I will be lost without her. The truth is that this department will go down fast without Shantelle, but Perkins has got me over a barrel. Until I can get a few loose ends tied up, there is nothing I can do. For the time being it is better to humor Perkins the more aggravated he gets, the harder things will get around here. You obviously don't want to follow my lead, but there are a few things that you need to keep in mind. I am still the boss. I do not have to tell you everything, and I do not have to explain myself to you. I do work on things that you know nothing about. What I do and the orders I give are done for good reasons. It is not your job to question my decisions. It is your job to follow orders. I put up with a lot from you because you are good. You are smart. You are creative, and you are usually reasonable. You are not being reasonable now."

"These so called policies are not reasonable," Jayson protested.

"No, they are not. I'm asking you to stop rocking the boat so much and be patient with me. I'm telling you, you will not deliberately disobey a direct order again. Do you understand?" Hawk pushed.

"Yes, sir," Jayson answered reluctantly.

"Get your assignment, and get out," Hawk instructed. He went back into his office and left Shantelle and Jayson alone.

"If you can find me something that won't take too terribly long, we can get something done about living arrangements when I get back," Jayson suggested.

"I won't be here when you get back," Shantelle reminded him.

Jayson looked a little confused. "Oh, that's right. Your two weeks will be up."

"I'll write my number down. Give me a call when you get back; I'll come up and help you do your report," Shantelle offered.

"Are you sure? You don't have to do that. I'm sure I can figure it out. Someone around here is bound to know how," Jayson returned.

"I doubt anyone will know how to do it, at least not at first. I'm the only one who has put a report on computer. Hawk has never even seen the program. It's not hard really. It won't take long to figure out if people are willing to sit down and play with it for a little while first. I can show you if you want, but I'm sure that I'll be bored out of my mind by the time you get back. I'm not the type to sit around and take it easy."

"Yeah, I can see that. Most people would not still be working this hard through their last two weeks after a pink slip. In fact I can't think of anyone who would," Jayson added.

"In other words, you think I'm weird," Shantelle translated.

"No, not weird. It's… it's… well, I don't know a word to describe you. You work harder than anyone up here, and you were rewarded with a pink slip. You don't owe them anything. No one would blame you if you sat back and let us fend for ourselves, but you don't. You're better than that. We could all learn a thing or two about work ethic from you and determination. Most of us could use a lesson in self control. I would be lashing out at the board with everything I could cook up."

"I am lashing back," Shantelle interjected.

"No, you're not, not really. You went along with my crazy, little scheme, but you're so calm. You're behaved. You've stood back all day. You haven't tried to rub it in. You haven't smarted off to anyone. You haven't gotten into mouthing matches with Perkins. You've been extremely well mannered. You've done everything that I couldn't. You are amazingly even tempered," Jayson bragged on Shantelle.

"That's not true. I'm boiling inside. I'm the type who keeps everything bottled up until I explode. Haven't you ever heard? We are the most dangerous kinds. You never know when we'll explode, but you do know that it will be horrific when we do," Shantelle described.

"Is that so? Have you ever exploded before?" Jayson inquired.

"Your assignment is on the printer. You better go on. Hawk will come out of his office for lunch sooner or later. I've never seen him this mad." Shantelle handed Jayson a sticky note with her name and number written down. "Give me a call when you get back. The assignment shouldn't take too long, but it won't be easy."

"Sounds like fun. I do love a challenge," Jayson said. He grabbed the assignment and was on his way.

Chapter Eight

It was almost two weeks before Shantelle heard back from Jayson. It was ten o'clock on a Thursday morning when he called.

"Hello," Shantelle answered.

"Hi, Shantelle? This is Jayson Black."

"Yeah, hi."

"I didn't wake you did I?"

"No, no, I'm a morning person. I've been up for hours."

"Great."

"Did you just get back?"

"I got back late last night. It was close to midnight. I didn't want to call that late."

"Thank you."

"Yeah, um, are you still interested in helping me with my report?"

"Yes, definitely. I'm ready whenever you are."

"That is awesome. I guess that I'll meet you back at the office in a couple hours."

"Perfect, I'll see you there."

Shantelle who is always punctual was at the office within an hour. On the other hand, it can be argued that Jayson has never been on time for anything in his life. It took Jayson two and a half hours to get to the office.

"Shantelle, am I dreaming?" Hawk exclaimed when he saw Shantelle walk into the office.

"No, you're not dreaming. I'm meeting Black, I mean Jayson, up here to help him out with his report. He called me this morning, got back last night," Shantelle replied.

"Oh, yeah, that's right. How are the newlyweds doing?" Hawk asked with a sarcastic look.

"How are things going around here?" Shantelle asked ignoring Hawk's question.

"Everything is awful. I'm going insane," Hawk admitted. "I can't find anything. My in box is stacked up three times as high as my out box. It takes me a lifetime to deal out assignments. I don't know how the reports are working out; I never have time to check them anymore. I stay so busy that I don't know how the assignments are being done or if they are even being done. I honestly have no idea what's going on anymore.

The phone rings off the hook all day long everyday. I never realized before how many phone calls we get. I can't keep the files up to date. I'm going to be lost if another department requests any information. I don't know what to do. It is going to take the board less than a year to destroy what took me fourteen years to build. Shantelle, I would love to stand here and catch up, but I have got to run, dear."

Hawk took off as the phone rang nonstop behind them. Shantelle looked around. Her desk could not even be seen anymore. It was covered over with files. Most of the files were confidential, on a need to know only basis. The stacks were as high as the computer. Hawk had obviously not filed anything since Shantelle left.

The waste basket was overflowing with waded up balls of paper. The shredder was set up in a corner on a tall rectangular wastebasket just as Shantelle had left it. Beside it was a stack of papers to be shredded. The stack was as high as the shredder itself; it was tipping to one side and looked like it would fall at any moment.

Shantelle started putting the files away one by one and was still filing when Jayson arrived. She had barely put a dent in the files when Jayson walked in.

"What are you doing? You don't work here any-more," Jayson reminded her.

"I know, but look at this place," Shantelle returned.

"It does look pretty bad in here," Jayson admitted.

"Do me a favor. Go over there and start shredding," Shantelle said gesturing to the corner where the shredder sat.

"Ugh, that will take all day," Jayson moaned.

"Please," Shantelle begged. "If not for me, do it for Hawk. I talked to him briefly when I got here. He is at his wits end. You can tell he's really worried."

Jayson walked over to the shredder without further argument. "I was looking forward to telling you about my assignment," he said as he started shredding papers. "It was awesome."

"Awesome, really?" Shantelle challenged. She knew that his latest assignment had to do with an illegal fighting rink.

"Yeah, as twisted as this may sound, I had fun," Jayson admitted.

"Really? I would have never guessed that about you," Shantelle responded.

"I wouldn't have either until I actually tried it," Jayson agreed. "I would never have done anything like that on my own. I mean, I can't see it being something I ever do again, but it was fun while I was there."

"It was illegal," Shantelle added.

"Really?" Jayson said sarcastically. "I must have missed that part. No, believe me. I paid for it. I'm still paying for it; I hurt so bad. Just between you and me, I think I've got a cracked rib. I'll be hurting for a while."

"Oh, I'm sorry," Shantelle reacted.

"Why? It's not you're fault," Jayson responded. "So, from the looks of it, I'd say things aren't going well." It was a feeble attempt to change the subject.

"I guess not," Shantelle agreed allowing the subject change.

"You said Hawk sounds worried?" Jayson inquired.

"Yeah, he said he can't keep up. He admittedly has not been checking the reports."

"That's not good. Now more than ever he needs to be checking over the reports. Not only to make sure they're right but when you were doing all the reports, you could alert him to any red flags immediately," Jayson pointed out.

"It was always important to Hawk that he knew exactly what was going on with his department. I feel so bad for him, especially since I know it's not his fault."

"It must be rough for him to watch his baby dying like this. He has put his heart and soul into this department. This is fourteen years of his life going down the drain. I can't imagine. I wish there was something I could do for him," Jayson sympathized.

"Getting this mess up will help. I don't know how anyone keys in a report. No one can get to the computer. Not to mention, most of these files are confidential.

They don't need to be sitting out for anyone to get their hands on. That stuff you're shredding wouldn't need to be shredded if it weren't confidential. If Mr. Foster came in here and saw this, he would have a cow. He is very big on keeping confidential information confidential."

"Foster, he's that tall guy who is always with Perkins, isn't he? What is up with him?" Jayson asked.

"What do you mean?"

"He's just real weird. He sits back to himself. He's real standoffish, never has too much to say. He never has an opinion of his own."

"A lot of people are shy," Shantelle interjected.

"Why join the board? If you have nothing to add, what's the point? I don't think that's what his problem is. He follows Perkins's lead in everything. He agrees with everything Perkins says. He always votes Perkins way."

"Maybe he latched onto Perkins as sort of a security blanket," Shantelle added.

"I don't think so. That's pretty far fetched even for someone who is shy. He would at least be hesitant on the issues he didn't agree with, especially issues as off the wall as these new policies. It's like he's Perkins' lap dog or a robot or something. I don't know. He's just weird. He has no mind of his own," Jayson argued.

"He may not be real confident yet. This really isn't his thing. This is a second job for him. He's a CEO at some big business. He's not use to this type of thing. This place still throws me from time to time, and I grew up in this world," Shantelle counteracted.

"I guess you've got a point, but my point is that he should not have taken the job if he couldn't handle it. He could have at least found someone better to latch onto."

"Okay, whatever," Shantelle gave up.

"You know, I think this is the most we've ever talked," Jayson commented.

"This is the longest you've ever stuck around," Shantelle pointed out.

"I've never had any reason to stick around before," Jayson replied.

"If I had thought I could get away with putting a board member to work shredding, I would have done it years ago. It's not a hard job; any idiot could do it. It is just so time consuming to sit there and feed it through, and it's confidential," Shantelle admitted.

"Oh, that's interesting. So, how long have you seen me as just another idiot?" Jayson asked, but Shantelle was saved by an opening door.

Hawk came out of his office and stared at Shantelle and Jayson. The stack of papers to be shredded had been cut in half, and Shantelle had almost completely cleared off the desk. Hawk smiled and said, "I thought you were here for a report."

"I couldn't leave that mess," Shantelle told him.

"Thank you both so much. I don't know what I would have done without you. I'm almost to the point that I need a bedpan in the office to save time."

"That was too much information," Jayson cracked.

"It was a joke, Black," Hawk corrected.

"I would be worried if it wasn't."

"I'm going to run to the restroom. Thank you," Hawk said, and he took off. He was almost literally running.

"He looks like he hasn't slept in days," Jayson commented.

"He probably hasn't. It wouldn't be the first time he's foregone sleep for this place. I think he averaged a night a week in the beginning," Shantelle recalled.

Chapter Nine

Shantelle was filling away the last folder when the phone started ringing. Hawk was still in the bathroom, and the rest of the floor was deserted. There did not appear to be another soul other than Shantelle and Jayson.

Shantelle walked over to the desk and picked up the phone. "Shantelle White... Yes, sir... I wouldn't know, sir... Neither, sir... Yes, sir, I'm fully aware... Of course not. I'll take care of it right away, sir... Yes, sir, right away..." Shantelle hung up the phone.

"You don't work here. What will you take care of?" Jayson accused.

"Something that has got to be taken care of ASAP to avoid a war," Shantelle answered.

"What!?" Jayson reacted as Hawk walked up.

Shantelle booted up the computer. "I just took a call from the head of national security," she told Hawk.

"What's up?" Hawk asked.

"Osborn is on the loose again."

"What has he done now?"

"It seems that this time he blew up an American embassy. It can't be proven that it was him. It was set up to look like a local terrorist group funded by the government, but Osborn can be placed there just one hour prior to the explosion. There are riots breaking out. The national security wants to know immediately if it was Osborn before they counteract. He said if we can find proof that it wasn't Osborn to call back ASAP; otherwise clean up the mess. I'm pulling up Osborn's file right now… He was on assignment in that area. His target was an employee at the American embassy," Shantelle reported.

"It does sound like Osborn," Hawk mumbled.

"I'm on it," Shantelle said.

"It's getting late, and you don't work here anymore. I can't ask you to do that," Hawk responded.

"You don't have to," Shantelle returned.

"You are the best. I owe you big time," Hawk bragged. "I don't even have to worry about that knowing that you are on the job."

"Wow, he really trusts you, doesn't he?" Jayson said once Hawk disappeared into the office again.

"I've dealt with Osborn before," Shantelle said.

"That's not what I mean. You've been pink slipped. You could be a disgruntled former employee bent on revenge," Jayson explained.

"I guess I could be. Can we talk about this later?"

Hawk interrupted on the intercom. "Shantelle, I don't have time to deal with anymore of Osborn's shenanigans, and this department can't take one more. Can you make sure that he takes a fall for this one?"

"Sure," Shantelle buzzed back

"Thanks," Hawk added.

"We need…" Shantelle mumbled to herself. She sat down at her computer and looked something up. Funny how it still felt like her computer. She picked up the phone and dialed. "This is Shantelle. You need to get to the office ASAP."

Shantelle hung up the phone and Jayson asked, "What was that about?"

Shantelle did not hear him at all. She was busy at the computer. She was focused. No more than five minutes later. Something started printing out. Jayson was almost through shredding. He kept working and did not bother Shantelle. She was in the zone, and Jayson had to respect that kind of diligence.

Shantelle worked on the computer another ten minutes then got the papers off the printer. Jayson had already finished shredding. He was gathering trash from around the room.

"Thanks," Shantelle said.

"No problem. You get seriously focused, don't you," Jayson commented.

"Yeah, I can, especially on something this important."

"Now what?"

"You can go home. I don't think we are going to get your report tonight. I've got to wait on Fox. I'm sorry I wasted your time," Shantelle apologized.

"It's no problem. I'm happy to help. Where are the night guardsmen?" Jayson asked.

"I don't know," Shantelle answered. "Sometimes Hawk will give them the night off when he knows he'll be here all night."

"Well, I'll just wait here with you," Jayson offered.

"You don't have to do that. I'll be fine. Hawk is here if I need him. I've already wasted enough of your time."

"Don't be silly," Jayson responded. "I wouldn't dream of leaving you here."

"It won't be long, I'm sure. Fox doesn't have that far to come," Shantelle said as the elevator started working. "I bet that's him right now."

The elevator opened up. A tall lanky man with dark hair stepped out. His hair was a disheveled mess. He needed a shave. He looked like he had just rolled out of bed, and he was holding a gun in his left hand.

"You can put the gun away, Fox," Shantelle said calmly.

Fox looked at her and smiled. "I'm glad to see you. I thought I was walking into a trap. It's the middle of the night, and I heard you had been let go."

"I was let go," Shantelle replied, "but this is sort of a state of emergency." She handed him the papers she had retrieved from the printer. "We need your expertise."

"You need me to plant evidence?" Fox asked.

"You have your assignment," Shantelle replied.

Fox glanced over at Jayson then back at Shantelle. He looked down and started to read over the assignment. "I don't understand. I thought he was one of ours."

"He is guilty. We want to make sure that he gets caught, and it's not your job to ask questions. If you can't do the job, I'm sure Black can," Shantelle threatened glancing at Jayson.

"I can do it," Fox said.

"Good, call in as soon as it's done," Shantelle instructed.

Fox nodded and left. "I didn't think you had it in you," Jayson commented out of no where.

"What is that?" Shantelle questioned.

"You really took charge. You were totally authoritative and no nonsense. I mean, I knew that you took no nonsense. I've witnessed that one first hand many times over, but I had no idea you could be so authoritative. It sounds like Hawk is beginning to rub off on you," Jayson accused.

"I'm not like that with everybody. You get to know the men. You learn what each one needs in order to be effective. Fox is super paranoid. He would stand here and question until morning if I let him. The more questions you try to answer, the more he thinks you're trying to hide something," Shantelle explained.

Hawk came out of the office and asked "Where are we?"

"Fox just came in to pick up his assignment. I've got him planting evidence. I left a tip with a local reporter. By the time he gets out there, Fox should have the evidence planted. Fox is supposed to call in as soon as his assignment is complete. If he gets the evidence planted correctly, then there is no way that Osborn can get out of it and no way it can be traced back here. An e-mail has already been sent to the head of national security with a helpful tip on how to catch Osborn," Shantelle reported.

"Fox... that was good thinking. That's why you're the best. I appreciate everything that you've done, but you've already done too much. Shantelle go home and get some rest," Hawk said with gratitude and an almost fatherly adoration.

"Will you be okay?" Shantelle asked Hawk.

"I'll be fine. You be careful. You will walk her to her car?" he asked Jayson.

"Of course, sir; she's my wife," Jayson replied.

Hawk pinned Jayson with a stare but said nothing.

Jayson walked with Shantelle through the building. "I can't believe that Perkins was stupid enough to let you go. You are invaluable to this department. Besides all the paper work, office work, etc. that you do, you know how to handle each agent on a personal level, and you know off the top of your head who has an expertise in what."

"Yeah, well, that doesn't save money, and I didn't come through with that grant," Shantelle combated.

"That shouldn't matter," Jayson said as they approached Shantelle's car.

"Money is always the bottom line, and I didn't secure it."

Jayson hated that she would even suggest something like that. There was so much to life that was much more important than money. Worse was that with Perkins, it was probably true. He did seem obsessed with the almighty dollar.

"So, do you want to try that report again tomorrow?" Shantelle suggested.

"Yeah, that sounds good. Do you want to meet around ten?" Jayson planned.

"Ten is fine. Don't be late," Shantelle instructed.

"I'll try."

"Don't try. You set the time yourself. Don't be late," Shantelle repeated.

"Yes, ma'am," Jayson responded.

Chapter Ten

The next day Jayson pulled into the parking lot close to ten seconds before Shantelle.

"Go ahead, and take note. I beat you here this morning," Jayson teased.

"I'll try to remember you were on time for once in your life," Shantelle shot back.

When Shantelle and Jayson got upstairs, there was already another agent on the computer.

"Shantelle, oh, thank heavens! You're back!" the agent exclaimed.

"I'm not really back. This is more of a visit," Shantelle corrected.

"Oh, I'm sorry," the agent apologized. "I can't get used to you not being here. Would you mind coming to read over my shoulder, just make sure I'm doing this right?"

Shantelle walked over behind the agent and looked at the computer screen. "Looks good so far."

"Thanks," the agent said. That was all the agent had to say.

Shantelle took a seat with Jayson to wait for the computer. "For someone who can't get used to you being gone, he doesn't miss you very much," Jayson whispered.

"What did you want, an emotional reunion?" Shantelle asked.

"Something indicating he missed you in the least."

"You don't get real close to people around here, and the men and women around here do not show a lot of emotion. He never said he didn't miss me," Shantelle pointed out.

"Okay, fine, I get it," Jayson relented.

No sooner than Shantelle and Jayson got to the desk, Osborn stormed in off the elevator. He slammed his palm down on the desk and shouted, "I want to see Hawk, now."

Shantelle did not say a word to Osborn, but Jayson did stand up and trying not to appear confrontational until he knew what was going on, put himself between Osborn and Shantelle. She buzzed Hawk's office and called, "Hawk?"

"Yes," Hawk answered.

"Osborn is here to see you."

"Send him in."

"You can go in," Shantelle told Osborn when he did not make a move.

"Did you have something to do with this?" he asked.

"No, sir, I did not," Shantelle answered.

"Why is this happening?"

"You were told not to use excessive force. You were told to keep things on the down low. You decided to blow up and American embassy," Shantelle recapped.

"I know the facts," Osborn growled.

Jayson slid a step to his right to further obscure Osborn's view of Shantelle.

"Shantelle, I said send him in," Hawk buzzed.

"I'm trying to, sir."

Hawk opened his office door and forcefully in-structed Osborn, "Get in here, now."

Osborn walked reluctantly into the office. "Wow, now, that is a disgruntled employee," Jayson commented.

Shantelle ignored Jayson. She picked up the phone, dialed quickly, and talked softly. "We've got Osborn here now, if you can get here in five minutes or less."

"Was that who I think it was?" Jayson asked when Shantelle hung up.

"Head of National Security," Shantelle responded.

"You know that number by heart?" Jayson questioned.

"You memorize all the emergency numbers when you're in a high risk job. It's a matter of survival."

"Wow, the more I learn about you, the more amazed I am," Jayson said in awe.

"Shhh," Shantelle hushed him.

"They can't hear us. There is a yelling match going on in there," Jayson pointed out.

"No, Osborn is doing all the yelling. Hawk can't get a work in edgewise," Shantelle whispered.

It did not take long for a team from National Security to arrive. They came in quickly and quietly. Shantelle pointed at the office door. The lead man nodded. He pointed at Shantelle and Jayson then pointed down the hall. Shantelle got up immediately to move down the hall. Jayson did not move as quickly. Shantelle grabbed Jayson's arm and pulled him down the hall with her.

"Where are we going?" Jayson asked in a whisper.

Shantelle put a finger to her lips. She turned into the ladies restroom and pulled Jayson in with her. She turned and flipped a deadbolt high on the door that Jayson was sure the men's room didn't have. He looked around and gave Shantelle a funny look. The restroom was empty with the exception of Shantelle and Jayson.

Shantelle slid up onto the counter backwards. "You might as well have a seat. We'll be here until we get the all clear from Hawk," she whispered.

"This is your version of getting out and to safety?" Jayson asked.

"This is the plan for this type situation," Shantelle answered, "but I've got to admit. I do feel better not being alone."

"I guess so," Jayson agreed. "Have you ever had to come in here before?"

"Oh yeah, this is the ladies restroom," Shantelle smarted back.

"You know what I meant," Jayson accused, but Shantelle did not respond. They were interrupted by a loud crash followed immediately by gunshots. A tremendous commotion and yelling continued for several minutes.

Shantelle and Jayson sat in the restroom for nearly an hour. When a knock sounded on the door, Jayson instinctively pulled his gun and aimed at the door.

"All clear," Hawk called through the door, but Jayson knew all too well how coercive a deranged lunatic could be. He kept his gun out and ready as he slowly opened the door.

"At ease," Hawk said when he saw the gun. "I'm glad to know you were here with her, but you can both relax now. It's all over, and Osborn is in federal custody."

Jayson gave Shantelle a hand down. "I'm glad I was here to alert National Security," she said.

"I am too," Hawk agreed. "Did ya'll get that report knocked out?"

"No, we had just sat down when Osborn came in," Shantelle answered.

"It really disturbs me that I don't know who's coming and going, but you know I can't work with my door open. I just can't work with the distractions you can," Hawk admitted.

"She's an amazing woman, isn't she?" Jayson said.

"Yes, she is," Hawk responded. "I just can't figure out how she got mixed up with you."

"Neither can I. Perkins has a way of getting to people," Jayson added.

"Yes, he does," Hawk agreed. "So, was this whole union really just a rebellion against the new policies?"

"Yeah, I'm afraid so," Shantelle answered morosely.

"Mmmm," Hawk shook his head. "I've got a lot of work to do. I'll see ya'll later," and Hawk went back to his office.

"Not one to mix words, is he?" Jayson poked.

"He doesn't like wasting time dancing around the truth," Shantelle replied.

"You know him better than I do. What was that about?" Jayson asked.

"He has a lot to do. He doesn't have the time to spend chit-chatting. A well placed grunt gets his point across," Shantelle answered smartly.

"What was his point?" Jayson asked almost sure of the answer.

"He was letting me know that he thinks we made a mistake."

"Hasn't he already done that?"

"Yeah, he has. Do you want to give that report another go?" Shantelle suggested. It was obvious that Shantelle did not want to talk about it, and it was also obvious that she had no intentions of discussing it any further.

"I guess we should," Jayson agreed.

Elizabeth Lee Sorrell

Chapter Eleven

This time there were no interruptions. Shantelle opened up the computer program and said, "Okay, tell me what happened."

"It was awesome. I loved it. That was actually a lot of fun," Jayson said.

"It was?" Shantelle reacted. Even though he had told her that once she still had trouble believing it.

"Yeah, I know that sounds awful, but I really did have fun on this assignment. I'm still sore, but it was totally awesome," Jayson continued.

"You know that wasn't a legal tournament, right," Shantelle checked. If he really did enjoy fighting as a sport there were other more legal ways to go about it.

"Oh, I know. I knew that going in," Jayson replied.

"I just can't imagine you enjoying something like that," Shantelle added.

"I never could either. It doesn't make good sense to fight like that and call it sport. I know there is boxing and wrestling. I've never been interested in either, but this is very different. This is pure fighting. It's almost no holds bars. There were very few rules, and if someone dies during a fight, oh well. They knew the risks going in."

"That's awful," Shantelle mumbled.

"Yeah, but it worked out well for us," Jayson reminded.

"I guess so," Shantelle relented. "So what happened?"

"How much do you need, just the round with my target or what?" Jayson asked.

"Tell me everything from the time you got there till the time you left," Shantelle instructed. Of course she needed it for the report, but he had her interest peeked now as well.

"Okay, well, I got there kind of last minute. They don't give a lot of notice since it is illegal. I got there only a few hours before it all started. I barely got signed up in time. I was jet-lagged, and I wasn't completely sure what I was getting thrown into. I knew it was an illegal fight tournament, but I seriously underestimated the intensity. Those men were out for the kill. They would try any underhanded trick they could think of.

"The guy I fought in the first round wasn't necessarily bad; he was a young kid, and we just weren't on the same level. It wasn't the best I had ever fought being jet-lagged and all, but I was making it. It was clear that I was going to win. The guy twisted around and dislocated my shoulder. I don't know why I let myself get in that position. I guess it was because I was tired. That was when I got my first taste of the intensity. It was just a tournament, a game. It was clear that this guy wasn't going to move on. He had to know that, but he still dislocated my shoulder on purpose. When he did that the crowd went nuts. This enormous crowd ignited when he dislocated my shoulder."

"You had your shoulder dislocated in the very first round?" Shantelle interrupted. "How many rounds were there?"

"Fourteen," Jayson answered.

"Oh my goodness, did you fight in all fourteen rounds?" Shantelle asked.

"Yes, do you want to hear the rest?" Jayson returned.

"Go on."

"I popped my shoulder back into place and found some ice before the next round. That wasn't easy. We were out in the middle of no where. It was about thirty miles out from the nearest town and in a big empty field. There were shoulder to shoulder people for at least a mile. Thank goodness the next two guys I faced went down quick and easy.

"The next guy was more show than anything else. That's not to say that he wasn't good. He was good, but he was too concerned with the crowd. He would get a good move in on me and then turn to face the crowd. He would completely turn his back to me. That's when I started hitting him, hard. Believe it or not, it took him three or four times before he figured out not to turn his back to me. By the time he quit turning his back to me, he was pretty much done for. It was only a matter of time from that point. Eventually he did give in before someone got seriously hurt.

"The next one was slow, but interesting. I wasn't sure at first if the guy was ever going to fight or if he was going to turn and run. We were doing a lot of dancing around. There were a lot of swings and misses. That was when I started to get in to it. This time it felt like a work out with a friend or colleague. I got an adrenaline rush, and we were off. I felt kind of bad when it was over. It ended with a knock out. He wasn't out long, just long enough for me to win. I didn't mean to. I didn't think I hit him that hard, but I must have. I did walk by his little group later to look in on him. He looked fine. He was flirting with a couple girls and bragging about making it to the fifth round.

"The next man was badly beaten from previous fights. He had no business still in it. He could barely move, but he wouldn't give up. He definitely had heart. I wasn't sure how to approach this guy. I didn't want to hurt him; he was already hurt enough, but I couldn't throw the fight either. I had to keep going until I got to our guy. I took it as easy as I could. The crowd knew it too. They were booing something terrible. That poor guy, there is no way that he avoided a hospital that night or that morning really.

"It was getting into the early morning hours now. I haven't had any sleep since before I boarded the plane, over two days ago, and now I've been in six different fights with one dislocated shoulder. I should have been dead on my feet. I was running on pure adrenaline, and I was pumped.

"The next guy wasn't all that great. He had very little skill. I was confused at first. There was no way that he had made it that far on nothing but dumb luck, but as we went on, I began to understand. He was determined and tough. It did not matter what I threw at him; he kept coming back. I don't know how the guy was still standing. I really don't. I all but killed him. He was a scrappy little guy. Scrappy enough that the fight wound up going long. He was exhausting me. That one ended with a knock out too, but I was just thankful to get that one over with. I was positive that guy had to go to the hospital, but do you know? I saw him later on. He was with another couple guys and a first aid kit. That guy is just too tough for his own good.

"The next guy was smart. He had been paying attention right from the get go. The first move he made was to go right after my sore shoulder. I was forced to fight defensively trying to protect that shoulder. He would take a jab at it every chance he got. I kept thinking that I had to get out of there fast, so I started fighting back that much harder. Man, I know I hurt that guy. I know I did. He was still conscious when it was over, but I didn't see him anymore. I felt so bad about that one, still do, but at the time I couldn't help my excitement for the next round.

"I don't remember much about the next round. I wasn't very focused. My shoulder was hurting, and that is all I really remember about it.

"The next guy, wow, he was huge. He was every bit of six-nine or six-ten. He was at least a head taller than me and almost twice as wide. I have never seen anyone that huge. Talk about intimidation. He intimidates by size alone, but you know what they say. The bigger they are the harder they fall.

"I knew the next guy from somewhere. I know I've seen him somewhere before. I just can't put my finger on where. I still can't, but I know I knew him. We were somewhat evenly matched too. It was a long match. I threw everything I had at that guy. He finally stayed down, but he took a lot before going down. Unfortunately I took a lot before he went down as well.

"I was so exhausted after that match, and there was very little down time between matches by this point. I still had not gotten to our target, but he was still in it. I had seen him in a few matches. He was good, and I was getting more exhausted and more beat up with each passing round. I was already black and blue, and I was barely moving between matches.

"I guess the next guy was desperate to win. I had heard him talking earlier. He was bragging that this was his third year, and he had made it to the top five every time. He said he was going all the way this time. Well, he didn't, but he did put up a good fight. Why is it that everyone wants to go for the ribs?" Jayson asked.

"It hurts. It knocks the wind out of you, and if they crack a rib, it makes it hard to breathe," Shantelle answered. She was listening intently and typing fast.

"He definitely cracked a rib, maybe a couple. Have you ever had a cracked rib? They take forever to heal. He went for my ribs right off the bat. He had apparently not been paying much attention to the previous matches, because he left my shoulder alone. It was just as well; he hurt my ribs bad, and he kept going for my kidneys. You have no idea how bad that hurts. This guy definitely fought dirty, and he got the drop on me. It took a lot to come back. I was in a lot of real pain. Somehow I came out on top. I honestly have no idea how. Afterwards all I could do was find somewhere off to the side and double over.

"I got some kid passing by to find me some ice. He actually came through with the ice; I really didn't think he would, but he did. I wasn't able to ice down my ribs long, and every breath was excruciating.

"Finally I got to our target. It took me till the thirteenth round to get to him. I was tired. I was in pain, and he was obviously good to have made it that far. He was good but not good enough. He made a tough go of it. This guy had skill. He was running on more than adrenaline. He had more than heart or desperation. It looked like the fight had potential to drag on forever. Neither of us could get a blow in on the other, not a substantial one anyway. For a long time every move was blocked and counteracted. He was favoring his left leg. I was favoring my right side and shoulder. At first everything was a fair fight, but when he took a shot at my shoulder, I went for his leg. I kicked at his left leg and knocked his good leg out from under him. He crumpled to the ground like a rag doll. I could see the pain written across his face. He was most likely fighting with a broken leg. It didn't take him long to jump back to his feet, but he was off balance. He was trying to keep the majority of his weight on his right leg. The slightest tip to his left sent him flailing to the ground. After that point it was all down hill for him. He was easy to take down, but he was also quick to get back to his feet. He tried to use upper body strength. He had the obvious advantage there, but a break was no match for a dislocation. I was in serious pain, but my injury was easier to fight through. The last time I got him down I was in a position that I could easily get to his neck. I threw my shoulder out again, but I snapped his neck, made it look accidental too.

"I completed my assignment, and I had moved on to the next round. It was the last round, the championship round."

"You finished the tournament, didn't you?" Shantelle interrupted with a slightly accusing tone.

"Yeah, I did," Jayson answered wide eyed.

"Weren't you already in enough pain?" Shantelle accused.

"Apparently not. I was so close. I had to finish."

"How did you do?"

"You are looking at the champion," Jayson announced. "The guy was so cocky. He came in with a big stupid grin. I guess he had the right to be cocky. After thirteen rounds he didn't appear to be all that beat up. He didn't have half the number of bruises I did, and he wasn't favoring anything. He had no mercy. He went straight for my ribs every chance he got, and after a jab to my ribs, while he had me off guard, he would go for that shoulder. I was tired, and I was fighting like I was tired. I had already completed my assignment, so I didn't have that driving force anymore. I was clearly the underdog this time. This guy was killing me. I quickly got the feeling that he would literally kill me if he got the chance. Now it became a fight for my life. It's amazing how you get a second wind when your life is on the line. I took the guy by surprise. He wasn't ready, and that made it easy. The first time I took him down after that, I slammed his head against the concrete, and that was all it took."

"Did you…"

"No, I didn't kill him. He's still alive and not in nearly as much pain as I am," Jayson said. "That's it. I stumbled away broken and half dead. I got cleaned up and got right back on a plane for home."

"Oh my goodness," Shantelle stammered. "And you enjoyed that?"

"Yeah, I know what you're thinking. I must be an idiot. It was such a rush though. I mean it's not the sort of thing I ever want to do again, but I'm glad I got the chance to experience it once," Jayson responded.

"Okay," Shantelle said and shut the computer down. "You must have healed fast. You don't look any worse for the wear."

"Looks can be deceiving. My clothes cover the bruises," Jayson told her.

"Mmm, have you been to the doctor?" Shantelle asked.

"Nah, there's really nothing they can do," Jayson said. "So, that's it? There's nothing else we need to do?"

"That's it," Shantelle replied.

"Are you not going to show me how to do that?" Jayson inquired.

"I can if you want me to. I just figured that I would come up to help with them," Shantelle answered.

"Oh, that's fine. That's great. I was afraid that would get old for you. Won't you have better things to do?" Jayson asked.

"Not really," Shantelle responded.

"You didn't find anything to occupy your time?" Jayson questioned. "I mean if you don't mind me asking," he quickly backtracked.

"I've been packing," Shantelle answered.

"Why have you been… Oh, I didn't mean to make the decision for you. I was going to brainstorm with you when I got back to find a workable solution," Jayson reacted.

"I'm fine. I don't see a lot of options right now. I'm just thankful you're willing to help me out. Are you sure you don't mind me moving in. Will I be in your way?" Shantelle wondered.

"Good grief, no. I'm rarely home. I come home, report in, pick up my next assignment, and I'm gone again. You'll really see what I mean when you get moved in," Jayson said.

"I do have a question though," Shantelle spoke up.

"Shoot," Jayson responded.

"What all do I need to bring? Should I get rid of most my stuff?"

"Why would you need to get rid of your stuff?" Jayson replied.

"How much room will there be? Stuff like my couch, the last thing you need is to try and squeeze two in," Shantelle explained.

"If you've got it, there is room. Bring it on," Jayson said confidently.

"Are you sure?" Shantelle checked.

"Sure I'm sure," Jayson commented. "There's a lot of big stuff, huh? I tell you what; I can get a moving truck this weekend and come by to help. We'll get your stuff moved in, and I'll come next week for my next assignment."

"That would be great."

"Okay, I'll give you a call later this week," Jayson said as Hawk walked out of his office.

"Shantelle, Perkins is on his way up here. If you are still here when he gets here would you let me know," Hawk requested.

"I'm out of here," Jayson reacted. "I have no desire to still be here when he arrives. I do not feel like messing with him today. I'll see ya'll later."

"No offence," Shantelle started, "but I would rather not be here when he gets here either."

"I completely agree, and I don't blame you. If I had any choice I would skip out of here as fast as I could," Hawk agreed with both of them.

Shantelle and Jayson walked out together and wasted no time getting out of the parking lot.

Elizabeth Lee Sorrell

Chapter Twelve

Jayson did not call until Friday afternoon. Shantelle was almost convinced that he had forgotten.

"I got a truck tomorrow from seven to seven," Jayson told her. "Could you be ready to start by seven-thirty?"

"I can. The question is can you," Shantelle returned rather saucily.

"Is that supposed to be insulting?" Jayson asked very calmly and nonchalantly. "I'll be there. See you tomorrow."

"Hey, don't you need directions, or an address or something?" Shantelle asked.

"I think I can find it. See you then." Jayson hung up before Shantelle had a chance to say anything else. She had never given him her address or hinted in any way to where she lived. How could he possibly find it?

Jayson got to Shantelle's by seven-twenty Saturday morning. He looked tired; he appeared only half awake.

"I don't even want to know how you know where I live," Shantelle commented when she opened the door.

"It's not as bad as you think," Jayson defended, but Shantelle ignored him. She continued on as if he had said nothing at all.

"You're on a roll. Today makes two."

"Two what?" Jayson responded. Shantelle held her watch up over her shoulder, implying that Jayson was on time, as she led him into the house.

"Yeah, well, after I picked up the truck, where was I going to go in that big tank?" Jayson joked.

The front room was full of boxes plus a couch, a recliner, a table, and an entertainment system. The kitchen was full of boxes. "I thought all the big appliances could stay like the fridge, stove, and dishwasher. It will help the house sell." Jayson nodded, but did not have much to say.

There was a large antiqued looking dinning table in the dinning room it was covered over with boxes, and boxes were stacked in the six oversized chairs.

In the bedroom, Shantelle had already taken the bed apart. There was a large chest of drawers. The mirror had been taken off of a nice sized dresser. There were two large quilts draped over the mirror. There was also a set of luggage and a ton of boxes in the bedroom.

"Is that it?" Jayson asked sarcastically.

"That's it."

"How does one person have so much junk?" Jayson poked.

"It could have been a lot worse. I'm not as bad as some people. In fact, I'm not a pack rat at all. You can't afford to be the way I was raised," Shantelle came back.

"That makes sense. I can totally sympathize with that one," Jayson mumbled almost under his breath.

"That's why I told you we don't have to take all the furniture," Shantelle continued.

"No, that's okay," Jayson responded. "There should be room for all of it. I don't want you to get rid of your stuff. You're already having to uproot; that's enough."

"Are you sure. I completely understand if I need to get rid of some of it. I don't want to overcrowd your house," Shantelle said.

"No, uh-uh, don't be ridiculous. I said it was fine; it's fine. You've got a nice house here," Jayson commented.

"Yeah," Shantelle said with a smile, "I like it, liked it. It's small, but it's a nice size for one person. I've enjoyed it, thank you."

"Ouch! If you're trying to make me feel bad, it's working. The guilt trip is effective," Jayson returned.

"That's not what I meant," Shantelle backtracked. "It was not my intentions to make you feel bad, honest. I am so sorry."

"If you say so. Lucky for me, I bounce back quickly. So, are you ready to get started?" Jayson asked.

"Yes, please, before I stick my foot in my mouth again," Shantelle replied.

Jayson chuckled and picked up the first box. It was labeled bathroom. "Are they all labeled?" he asked.

"Yeah."

"Wow, you've really been busy. Are you always this organized in everything you do?"

"It will save time later, and besides I had nothing better to do," Shantelle admitted half defensively. "Do you always ask so many questions?"

"You never know, if you don't ask, and you'll never get to know some people if you don't ask questions," Jayson responded. He picked up a second box and walked out. Shantelle picked up a box and followed him out.

Not much else was said while they loaded the truck. Both Shantelle and Jayson worked diligently. The truck was one of the largest that the rental company had. It took only a little over an hour to load the truck. The truck held almost all of the boxes in the first load.

Jayson was sweating profusely. Sweat was already soaking through his shirt before they left with the first load. They had been working very hard. Shantelle was "glistening" a good bit herself.

Jayson closed the back of the truck. Then he and Shantelle climbed in to the cab of the truck.

"Do you know how to drive this thing?" Shantelle questioned.

"I got her over here just fine," Jayson shot back sharply. He was obviously tired.

"Well excuse me for asking," Shantelle reacted. "I was just curious if I should go ahead and take a deep breath now."

"That depends on what kind of passenger you are. It's not that far from here anyway."

Jayson was right. His house was only twenty minutes from Shantelle's, and he was a fairly decent driver, even in such an unusually enormous truck.

Jayson took Shantelle inside to show her around before they started unloading. The house looked extremely nice from the outside. It was a large brick home. It had a classic look and was obviously well cared for as well as the lawn. Jayson must have had someone who came to care for the lawn. He certainly didn't have time to keep a lawn this nice with his busy schedule.

From the inside, it looked shockingly bare. The living room was practically empty. There was one recliner and a twenty inch TV sitting in the floor. The kitchen was equally as empty. Aside from the major appliances, there really was not anything else to speak of. The dinning room looked like it had not been set foot in since the house was built; there was not a single item in the room. The half-bath had a single bar of soap and a single towel. The halls were drab walkways void of all signs of life. Every room was painted the same dull, beige color.

Jayson took Shantelle into the front bedroom. "This will be your bedroom."

The bedroom was spacious with a walk-in closet. It opened up into a private bathroom with a whirlpool jet tub, a walk-in shower, and a separate commode area. Shantelle looked around with astonishment. "This is the master bedroom, isn't it?"

"I liked the back room better," Jayson explained. He took Shantelle to the back room, his bedroom. "This is my room." There was not a whole lot more in his bedroom than any of the other rooms. There was a simple bed frame with a mattress and spring set. There was a large chest of drawers, but there could not have been much in the drawers. There were dirty clothes flung all around the room. As Shantelle looked around the room, the horror was evident in her eyes. She was used to organization. She kept her living space as neat and tidy as she did her work space, and his space was driving her crazy all ready. She had an overwhelming urge to start straightening up.

Shantelle and Jayson walked back to the front of the house, and she was struck again by how utterly vacant everything was here. "This is a joke, right?" Shantelle inquired. "You don't live here."

"No joke," Jayson said simply.

"This place is empty. You can't possibly live here," Shantelle argued.

"I'm not home much. There's no need for a lot of stuff. I tried to tell you there would be plenty of room for your stuff," Jayson explained.

"This isn't a home; it's a house," Shantelle blurted before she thought.

"Thanks," Jayson responded with a laugh.

"I'm sorry. I shouldn't have said that out loud. I'm tired," Shantelle apologized.

"No, I would rather you say what you're thinking than to humor me. You're right anyway. Hey, that will give you something to do, for a while at least. You can turn this house into a home," Jayson suggested.

"We'll see. Let's get everything unloaded for now."

It took an hour and a half to unload the truck and get each box to the correct room. After the last two boxes, Jayson went to the kitchen to get a cold, bottled water. "You want one?" he asked Shantelle as he tossed it to her without waiting for an answer.

It took a total of three trips and all day to get everything moved. Once the truck had been returned, Shantelle sat down on the couch to rest for a minute. They wound up both falling to sleep right there on the couch.

Chapter Thirteen

Jayson was the first to wake up the next morning at eight-fifteen. "Oh, I've got to get ready," he reacted.

"Where are you going?" Shantelle asked.

Jayson looked at her like he did not understand the question. "Church," he said. "Do you not go to church anywhere?"

"No, that's not the way I was raised." Jayson's reaction to Shantelle's simple statement was anything but simple. It is both interesting and inspiring to think about how many different thoughts can be given off from a single look. Jayson's look was: shocked, confused, sympathetic, concerned, reproachful, and calm. "Don't look at me that way. It's not what you're thinking. I am a Christian," Shantelle continued. "I was definitely raised in a Christian home, but we moved around a lot. It was impossible to find an actual church home. The way I was raised, I was taught that you don't have to be in a church pew every Sunday to be a Christian."

"I can understand that. I'm not at church every Sunday, far from it. I'm away working so much, but you're not. You've been pretty much grounded here for fourteen years. I know you don't have to be at church every Sunday to be a Christian, but I do believe that as a Christian, if the opportunity presents itself you should try to find a church home. That's something that's important to me. I have a church home. It's a part of keeping the Sabbath holy, you know? I'm not here much, but when I am, I'm at church. If you'd like to, I would really like for you to come with me," Jayson offered.

"Sure," Shantelle agreed cautiously.

The church building was big and beautiful. Shantelle had passed it everyday on her way to work but never paid attention. The building was a beige, brick building. The front porch had six columns going across and three sets of double doors. The foyer had elegant tile flooring. The sanctuary had astonishing stain glass windows. There were six down each side of the sanctuary with bright, bold colors.

When Shantelle and Jayson walked through the doors, they were met by the biggest smile ever seen. It was an overwhelming smile. It grabbed Shantelle's attention and held it, made it impossible for Shantelle to notice who, or what for that matter, was holding up such an astonishing smile.

"Jayson Black, two weeks in a row. To what do we owe this pleasure?" the smile said.

"I've had a little time off," Jayson answered.

"I'm certainly glad you have. I'm Robin Peace," the smile said to Shantelle who was still staring in wonder. "Are you a friend of Jayson's?"

"Something like that," Shantelle responded with an unsure cough.

Jayson rolled his eyes with a grin. "This is my wife, Shantelle. Shantelle, this is Robin," he introduced.

"Your wife? When did you get married?" Robin asked.

"A couple weeks ago or so," Jayson answered vaguely.

"Wow, the secretive life of a very secretive man," Robin commented. "I'm kidding. He is a secretive man, but I am very happy for both of you. And, I'm delighted you could come this morning. Are you coming to us from another church?"

"Oh, um," Shantelle stuttered.

"She hasn't been able to find a permanent church home yet. This is her first time visiting here, however," Jayson jumped in. It was a good thing too, because Shantelle was floundering. Give her a raging agent any day, but she was clueless against this woman and her sweet smile.

Just then someone called Robin from the other side of the foyer. "I'm sorry. I'll see ya'll a little later," she said.

"Thanks," Shantelle whispered to Jayson.

Jayson raised his eyebrows quickly and smiled. "She means well."

"I know. She seems very sweet," Shantelle replied.

All morning long people were surprised to see Jayson and eager to meet Shantelle. Shantelle met many interesting people and many kind people. Everyone she met made her feel welcome, and several spoke with her like as though she had been going there all her life.

"So what did you think?" Jayson asked on the way back to the house.

"It was nice," Shantelle admitted. "The people were all very nice. I really liked the music. I knew most of the songs."

"You knew most of the songs?" Jayson interrupted.

"Yes, I have actually heard Christian music before. I told you I was raised in a Christian home… You don't think very highly of me, do you?" Shantelle accused.

"It's not that at all. You read into things too much. I've never heard hymns anywhere outside church, well, very rarely anyway," Jayson clarified.

"You don't pay much attention. You can hear hymns outside church. Plus my mother used to sing hymns all the time when I was growing up. As for the contemporary music, I do have a radio," Shantelle commented.

"I know. I noticed that exceptionally heavy stereo system yesterday," Jayson returned.

"The preacher was real good too. It is different hearing a sermon live and in person," Shantelle added.

"I imagine so," Jayson replied.

The next day Jayson went to get his next assignment and he was off again. Shantelle started work on unpacking. It took noticeably longer to unpack than it had to pack. The days flew by. Jayson was gone for almost two weeks, and it took Shantelle the entire time to unpack.

Elizabeth Lee Sorrell

Chapter Fourteen

Only one day shy of two weeks to the day Jayson left, Shantelle was up getting breakfast and enjoying the serenity of aloneness. "Good morning," she heard. She screamed and jumped; then she grabbed a butcher knife off the counter and held it in front of her defensively.

"Hey, calm down. I got home last night," Jayson spit out quickly.

Shantelle let out a deep breath that she had been holding. She laid down the knife.

"Wow, you're jumpy. Not that I blame you for someone in your position," Jayson said. "Two precautions real quick. Number one, you need to be more aware of your surroundings. I got here last night; you should have known I was here by now, or at least known that someone was here. Number two, if I had a gun, that knife wouldn't do you much good. Next time assess your attacker before you react rashly."

"I'll try to remember that the next time I'm scared mindless," Shantelle came back.

"You do that. What are you doing up so early?" Jayson asked.

"I'm always up this early. What are you doing up this early?"

"I've got to get ready for church. By the way, you look nice."

"So do you."

"Why are you so dressed up?" Jayson asked slyly.

"Probably for the same reason you are."

"You didn't know I was back?"

"Nope."

"Have you been going to church while I was gone?"

"Yeah, I'm going to join this morning."

"Really? That was a quick decision. It looks like I got back just in time."

Shantelle and Jayson got to church early. Shantelle was exceptionally eager to get there. The sanctuary was half full. Shantelle and Jayson were both talking, each to different groups. Shantelle turned around and happened to notice Jayson's left side.

Jayson's shirt was turning deep, crimson. The crimson was around three inches in diameter, and the edges were quickly expanding. The crimson was visibly saturated even from five rows back.

Shantelle walked up to Jayson and leaned into his left shoulder. "You're bleeding... badly," she whispered.

Jayson walked away from the group with Shantelle. "I must have busted it open. It's a long gash. I've got to get out of here. If I don't stop the bleeding and get it re-bandaged, it's going to get ugly. I think it needs stitches."

Shantelle followed Jayson out of the church. They practically ran out and did not stop for anything.

"I'm so sorry," Jayson apologized once they were in the car and on their way.

"It's okay. Where are you going?"

"Home."

"Why are you going home? You need a doctor," Shantelle protested.

"I'll go. I'm going to take you home first."

"No, you are bleeding too much. Turn around, and go to the doctor now. You can take me home later," Shantelle argued with authority.

"Yes, ma'am," Jayson said and made a quick U-turn.

When they got to the hospital, the doctor who normally handles the agents was out of town on vacation. Jayson was forced to see someone else.

The gash was much worse than Jayson had described. The nurses took him back immediately to see a doctor. Jayson stayed in the back for three hours and forty-five minutes.

When he came out, he was moving slowly. "What did the doctor say?" Shantelle asked anxiously.

Jayson held up his car keys and dropped them into Shantelle's hand as he spoke. "He said you drive."

Shantelle asked again when they got into the car. "What did the doctor say?"

"Twenty stitches, and a ton of questions," Jayson answered.

"Oh my goodness! Twenty?" Shantelle reacted.

"Yeah, it sounds like I'm going to be out of commission for at least two weeks. My regular doctor will be back next week. We'll know better when he gets back. He's more familiar with my personal situation and my past history."

"He's also been debriefed on what all your job could entail," Shantelle added.

"That too."

"So what kind of questions did the doctor ask?"

"He wanted to know what happened. Nothing fit together, and it sounded like foul play. The wound was obviously from a knife, and my story was obviously bull."

"What was your story?"

"I fell. I slid across the sharp edge of a rock, and I was too macho to admit I needed a doctor until now."

"You're right. It's obviously bull. So, what really happened?"

"It's a knife wound from an attack I didn't see coming."

"You didn't see it coming?" Shantelle tested.

"That's what I said," Jayson reacted defensively. "I didn't see it coming. I was ignoring that person. It was a stupid mistake, and I paid the price."

"I didn't mean it accusingly. I was surprised that anyone could get the drop on you. That does make better sense though. You didn't view the attacker as a potential threat."

"No, I didn't," Jayson admitted disappointedly.

"That's nothing to be ashamed of," Shantelle grinned. "You're still one of the best I've met."

"One of?" Jayson challenged teasingly.

"Well, I've met a lot of agents," Shantelle pointed out.

"Okay, so what you're saying is that there is room for improvement. I can handle that. I'm not done yet. I'll blow your mind before it's all over."

"Uh-huh, I'll hold you to that," Shantelle said sarcastically.

Elizabeth Lee Sorrell

Chapter Fifteen

The next day Shantelle went with Jayson to the office to report in. Hawk was in his office with the door closed when they arrived. The computer was free, so Shantelle and Jayson got to work.

"Tell me when you're ready," Jayson said as Shantelle booted up the computer.

"Okay, shoot."

"Alright, my plane landed. I started asking around. I always start by asking questions. You never know what information someone might volunteer if you don't ask. You just have to be careful what questions you ask and who you ask. I found his girlfriend. She was a sweet little girl, young girl. She led me right to our guy. She appeared to be so shocked when it all hit the fan. I still believe that she had no idea. Anyway, he tried to flee. A struggle ensued. We ended up in the kitchen. I easily had the upper hand. This guy was out of shape. I got

Elizabeth Lee Sorrell

him pinned up against a counter and dug my forearm into his neck. This whole time I'm ignoring his hysterical girlfriend. I figured I could deal with her after I handled my target. He starts struggling to breathe. Then his girlfriend picks up a butcher knife and sliced into my side. I grabbed her hand and pulled it backwards. She lost her grip on the knife. I plunged it into the target. When I turned back to the girlfriend, she screamed and passed out. I dialed an ambulance for her and left them both with the phone off the hook. He's dead. I don't know how things will turn out for her. She was so hysterical she may or may not remember what happened, but her prints are all over the knife I used to kill him. Is there any way we can check on that? I don't want her taking the fall."

"I can make a couple phone calls. Let me save this, and I'll take care of that," Shantelle replied.

"Thank you," Jayson said. He walked over to the corner where the shredder sat and started shredding documents that were stacked all around.

Shantelle glanced over at Jayson and grinned then finished out his report. After Shantelle finished the report, she picked up the phone. She was barely on the phone for ten minutes. "Okay," she started to explain as she began filing folders stacked up in the floor. "She has been charged with his murder. Although there are still a lot of unanswered questions, there was enough evidence to charge her. I called a federal police group over there

122

that we have contact with. I told them that I could not tell them how he died or by whose hand, but I could tell them with definite certainty that it was not by her hand. They thanked me and said that they would handle it. She should be released by the end of the day."

"Shantelle, you are the best. I hate to think she would have been locked up for nothing, or worse what I did."

"Jayson Black, you are soft," Shantelle accused.

"I don't want other people to take my blame. How does that make me soft?" Jayson asked.

"Why won't you take any cases involving women targets?"

"I have trouble doing what has to be done with women targets," Jayson admitted.

"You're soft."

"Why should you care? You know you're immune no matter what you do or what path I take," Jayson shot back defensively. Shantelle had no doubt stumbled across a sensitive subject with Jayson. What had started out teasing had turned into something ugly in no time.

"Calm down. I never said it was a bad thing. If the truth be told, I personally think it's chivalrous that you can't kill a girl," Shantelle replied.

"Chivalrous? Where are we, stuck in medieval times?" Jayson came back.

"Sure, Black, try to act tough, but I know you have a sweet side."

"You said soft earlier," Jayson pointed out.

"So what? What's the difference?"

"There's a big difference. You can be sweet at times without being soft. Being soft in this business can get you killed," Jayson explained.

"Okay, fine. Have it your way, tough guy," Shantelle surrendered. "How's the shredding coming?"

"I'm done, just waiting on you."

"Great, I've got two files left. Give me one more minute."

Shantelle and Jayson left without ever seeing Hawk.

"I know it's none of my business, but you are the one who told me that if I don't ask, I'll never know. Have you ever killed a girl?" Shantelle asked.

"You're right. It's none of your business," Jayson said sternly.

"I'm sorry." Shantelle was sorry she ever brought it up as soon as she saw the look on Jayson's face. He looked hurt, deeply, and full of regrets. Shantelle had stumbled onto more than just a touchy subject; she had stumbled onto pain, long lasting pain with a firm hold.

"I did tell you that…" Jayson owned up to reluctantly after a moment.

"That's okay. I don't want to upset you. You don't have to dredge up painful memories."

"It is painful, but I don't have to dredge up any-thing. It's still fresh on my mind. I still think about it all the time. I did kill a woman once. I didn't like it, and I don't ever want to do it again. What I did still haunts me to this day. I've tried a million times to rationalize it in my head. I know so many other agents who can rationalize it in their heads, but I can't. I can't justify killing a woman for any reason. She was evil. She was really evil. She was supporting known terrorist groups. She was helping known terrorist into the country. She had her hands in a lot of other stuff too. The list goes on and on. She was smart. She was evil. She had to be stopped. It was my job to stop her. My bosses did not want her brought back alive. They wanted her disposed of. I did my job. I stopped her. Not a day goes by that I don't regret it. She was evil, but I still can't make that justify killing a woman. Since then I have proven myself as an agent. I can set my own limits or standards. I say I don't kill women, and people listen now."

"I'm sorry. I shouldn't have asked."

"If you don't ask, you'll never know, but don't tell anyone. That is my Achilles heel. I can be put up against almost anything, but all they have to do is send a woman after me. I melt. I may not always be the person I should be. I may do some lousy things where women are concerned, but I just can't kill a woman."

Shantelle looked at Jayson with a half curious half retentive expression which made Jayson very uncomfortable.

"I see you found the washer and dryer," Jayson said changing the subject. "My room was clean when I got home. I'm sorry. I meant to show you the basement. I just forgot."

"Don't worry about it. I can understand why you forgot. There's not much down there, your personal gym and a washer and dryer that has hardly been used. Have they ever been used?"

"Yes, I've used it. I use it every time it becomes a necessity."

"A necessity? You were about to that point, weren't you?" Shantelle teased.

"Yeah, I was," Jayson admitted. "You've been dying to do that though."

"What? I've been dying to do your laundry?" Shantelle challenged.

"You've been dying to clean that room. It was written all over your face the first time I showed it to you. It made you cringe."

"Okay, smart guy."

"Thank you… The house really is looking good. It's actually starting to look like a home. Don't you think?"

"Yeah, it's getting there."

Chapter Sixteen

Early Thursday morning Jayson was no where to be found. Shantelle was doing laundry again. She took the first load downstairs and found Jayson. He was working out lifting weights.

"What do you think you are doing?" Shantelle attacked.

"I'm going stir crazy around here. I've got to do something."

"Look harder," Shantelle instructed. "You can't do that. You're going to rip apart your stitches. Find something better to do."

"Yes, Mother," Jayson taunted.

Shantelle turned to the washer and dryer and started working on laundry. Jayson walked up behind her. "Are you cleaning again? You seriously can't stand disorganization, can you?"

"No, I can't," Shantelle admitted. She turned around and grinned at Jayson. That was when she noticed his side. "Now, see there. You're bleeding."

"Great," Jayson mumbled.

"Don't act so shocked. What did you think was going to happen? I've got a first aid kit upstairs in my bathroom. Come on, and we'll take a look at it."

Shantelle and Jayson walked upstairs to her bathroom. Jayson walked very gingerly now that the damage had already been done. Why he couldn't have been more cautious before he ripped apart his stitches was beyond Shantelle. She took out the first aid kit, and Jayson took his shirt off.

"You're blushing," Jayson laughed.

"Why would I be blushing, Black?" Shantelle returned. "You're not the first guy I've seen without his shirt, and in my line of work, you're definitely not the first six pack I've ever seen."

"So, you noticed my six pack."

Shantelle ignored his comment. She sat down on the toilet lid and started to saturate a cotton ball with alcohol. "Come here."

Jayson walked over in front of Shantelle, and she started dabbing away the blood with the cotton ball. "Will wonders never cease?"

"What?"

"It's bleeding from the edges. Somehow you managed not to tear a single stitch, but don't try that again.

You were lucky this time; you may not be so lucky next time. Quit flinching."

"It stings."

"You are a big baby for such a tough guy."

"Have you ever done anything besides the secretarial side of the job?" Jayson asked curiously.

"What do you mean?"

"Have you ever been asked to kill someone?"

"Good grief, no! I couldn't handle that sort of thing," Shantelle reacted.

"Owe, easy," Jayson flinched.

"Oh, you take it easy," Shantelle replied. "You can take a slash to the side, but you can't take someone cleaning your side with alcohol... Why would someone ask me to kill someone? I could never do something like that. I thought about being a nurse when I was younger. I wanted to help save lives, not take lives."

"Why don't you?"

"When my parents died, I had no money. I needed a job. When I got a job, I still didn't have money and then I didn't have the time either," Shantelle explained.

"You've got the time now. You've got nothing but time. Why don't you get a nursing degree now?"

"Now I have no job again."

"I do," Jayson pointed out. "I think there's enough money. We might have to make a few cut backs, but I think we could still make it easily. I mean we are a lot better off than I think you realize. We only barely couldn't make ends meet with two houses. Now that we are in one house, we are in a real good place financially."

"Whoa, whoa, just stop. I couldn't take your money to go to school," Shantelle interrupted.

"Our money," Jayson corrected. "It was my understanding that was part of the agreement. We get married partly so that you don't have to worry about money. How are you not going to worry about money if you are afraid to touch it?"

"Stuff like that is different. It's extra," Shantelle disputed.

"Oh yeah, you're right. It is different alright. You could better yourself. It could help you financially in the long run. Besides that, you might be happier," Jayson argued.

"I just wouldn't feel right about it," Shantelle insisted.

"I won't feel right until you feel comfortable with it, and I don't give up easily," Jayson forewarned.

"Neither do I."

"On the contrary," Jayson came back, "it sounds like you give up very easily. You said you wanted to be a nurse. How long did it take you to give up on that? You're not fighting for it very hard. I can understand that there were circumstantial blockades before, but now you've got all the opportunity in the world. Why are you still making excuses, lame excuses? Stop making excuses, and fight."

"You have an odd way of looking at things."

"I have an optimistic way of looking at things," Jayson corrected. "I don't know how you can have such a negative view of this. All I see is a win-win situation. What is stopping you?"

"I guess there is nothing stopping me," Shantelle relented.

"Great, so there's no problem here."

"No problem," Shantelle repeated. "We won't have a problem if you quit over doing it with these stitches."

"I'll try."

Jayson walked around the house all day Friday and Saturday griping about boredom. "Agggh, I'm going nuts. I can't sit here. I can't handle taking it easy." Saturday Jayson asked, "Aren't you bored? I'm bored out of my mind. What do you usually do on weekends?"

"I usually stay around the house. I spent the past fourteen years on call every weekend."

"You're kidding. That's pathetic. You're not on call anymore. I think that makes it time to get a life."

"Thank you a lot," Shantelle shot back sarcastically. "What do you usually do?"

"Sleep," Jayson answered simply. "I am more of a night owl, or at least I was until you came along."

"Sorry, what would you do on a typical Saturday night at home?"

"Um… nothing I would consider still doing."

"Okay, stop," Shantelle interrupted. "I don't want to go down that road again."

"What road would that be?" Jayson asked with a sly grin.

"Last time I asked you something you were hesitant to tell, I felt terrible in the end for asking in the first place."

Jayson looked disappointed. "Oh, is that all? I thought you had a good story to tell for a change," he teased.

Shantelle smiled. "We can't all be as interesting as field agents with a night life."

Shantelle curled up in her recliner, and Jayson stretched out in his. Shantelle flipped through the channels until she found a movie they could both agree on. The movie did not go off until two, and Shantelle started flipping through the channels again when the doorbell rang repeatedly.

Shantelle looked over at Jayson with a funny expression.

"Are you expecting company?" Jayson asked.

"At two in the morning, not hardly."

The doorbell rang repeatedly for a second time.

"I'm not answering that," Shantelle announced. "Two in the morning, at a field agent's house, there is no way I'm answering the door when I have no idea who's on the other side." Shantelle could not help the growing paranoia. There was nothing about the situation that could be good.

"I've got it," Jayson said getting up. The doorbell began ringing repeatedly again as he unlocked the door.

When Jayson opened the door, a busty, bleach blond, young girl fell in the doorway. Jayson stumbled back a couple steps as the girl fell into his arms.

"Jayson! Where have you been?" she cried. She was obviously drunk. Her speech was slurred, and she could barely stand on her own. Jayson helped her back to her feet. "I haven't seen you in at least a month and a half, maybe more. We've missed you. We've all missed you. Come on. Let's go play."

"I'm going to have to pass," Jayson turned her down.

"Okay, we don't have to go anywhere. We can play here just me and you," the girl offered as she pulled her shirt over her head.

"No, no, Ginger, put your shirt back on. You don't understand. I don't want to go play. I don't want to stay here and play. I don't want to play anymore. I'm married now. See, right over there," Jayson said pointing at Shantelle. "That's my wife, Shantelle."

"Jayson Black, married? I don't believe it!"

"It's true."

"No, it can't be true. You're the biggest player ever. Jayson Black does not settle down with any girl." The girl was very insistent now.

This was just great, Jayson scowled. This wasn't fair to Shantelle to have to watch this display, and she definitely didn't need to hear it. She was his wife, and that should be respected, no matter what their actual relationship was.

"Okay, Ginger, how did you get here?"

"There's a cab waiting," she slurred.

"Okay, get back in the cab. Go home. Sleep it off. Then spread the word; I'm out," Jayson instructed.

"Oh, pooh," the girl sighed. She turned and walked into the door frame.

Jayson rolled his eyes and told Shantelle, "I'll be right back." He helped Ginger into the cab, spoke to the cab driver, and sent them off.

Shantelle watched from the door. The girl, Ginger, was a sloppy drunk. She was hanging all over Jayson, and still couldn't manage to stay on her own two feet. Ginger was a part of Jayson's past, a past that didn't involve Shantelle. Ginger was none of Shantelle's business. It wasn't like Shantelle and Jayson had an intimate marriage either, but she still couldn't stop the twinge of irritation at Ginger's presence.

Shantelle was still waiting in the doorway when Jayson got back. He walked through the door sliding past Shantelle. "So you're a ladies man, huh?" she smiled.

"Was, I was a ladies man," Jayson corrected.

"Awe, don't let me spoil your fun. You can still go out, you know. I wouldn't stop you."

"No, I can't. I can't go out any more. I did a lot of fooling around when I went out."

"That's your decision," Shantelle said putting her hands up in the air.

"Yes, it is. It's my decision, and I take marriage very seriously. For whatever reason we entered into marriage, we are married now, and I'm not an adulterer," Jayson said seriously.

"Okay... I'm going to walk away now. You're making me uncomfortable. I have no idea how to react to that," Shantelle said nervously. It was obvious that Jayson had taken this whole marriage more seriously than she had. As far as she had been concerned, it was a partnership to get back at the policy board until she got back on her feet.

Jayson took a deep breath and sighed as she walked away.

Chapter Seventeen

The next day Shantelle was once again eager to get to church. This time there were no distractions, no unexpected emergencies. Shantelle finally got the opportunity to join the church at the end of the service.

Jayson was asked to come stand next to Shantelle, and after the service everyone walked by to shake their hands and hug their necks. Everyone expressed their excitement that Shantelle joined the church and pointed out how much more they've seen Jayson since he and Shantelle had gotten married.

It was a very quiet week at the house. Shantelle walked around nervously not saying much. Jayson tried unsuccessfully to ignore that there was a problem.

Wednesday Jayson went back to see his personal doctor.

"What did Dr. Hanson say?" Shantelle asked when Jayson returned home.

"He said I'm out of commission for at least another two weeks. I go back in two weeks, and he'll reevaluate it. He said it's still oozing blood and stuff. I need to keep it cleaned and fresh gauze." Jayson rolled his eyes and said, "I can't even reach the whole thing."

"I can help you keep it clean. It's still oozing? So, it's pretty bad, huh?" Shantelle commented.

"Yeah, I guess. Apparently it wasn't a real clean knife she slashed me with."

"He said it was oozing blood and stuff? What is stuff? Is it infected?"

"I don't know. He just said blood and stuff."

"Didn't you ask any questions?" Shantelle pushed.

"Yeah, I did. I asked when I could go back to work."

"Don't you think getting your side healed up should be first priority?" Shantelle continued to push.

"Maybe you should go with me next time so that you can get the four-one-one," Jayson shot off. He was frustrated with remaining on the DL, and Shantelle was the closest one to lash out at.

"Maybe I will if that's an offer."

"Great, that's just great," Jayson growled.

"What is your problem?" Shantelle demanded.

Jayson grunted and turned away. "Black, I asked you what your problem is," Shantelle repeated forcefully.

Jayson whirled back around to face Shantelle he was red faced, and his whole body way tense. "You want to know what my problem is," he shouted. "I hate waiting. I'm sick and tired of being bored. I want to work."

"Are you hungry?" Shantelle asked out of the blue.

"What?" Jayson could not hide his confusion.

"Are you hungry? Let's go get something to eat," Shantelle suggested.

"Right now?"

"Yes, right now. You're bored. You need to get out of the house. Let's go get something to eat and take the chance to calm down."

"Okay," Jayson agreed unconvincingly.

Jayson got in the car and asked, "Where are we going?"

"Wherever you want. Where is your favorite place to eat when you are at home?"

"That would be Mike's Bar-B-Q hands down."

"Where?"

"It's a small place off the beaten path. They have the best bar-b-que you'll ever put in your mouth."

"Okay, sounds great. Let's go."

Once they got their food and got seated Shantelle asked, "What do you like about your job?"

"I'm good at it. I like the challenge, but most of all I'm helping my country," Jayson answered.

"Is that a smile and maybe even a little pride I see?"

"No."

"Do you feel better?"

"No."

"Are you more relaxed?"

"Yes."

"That's something. We're making progress. What do you expect? I don't have a background in psychology… This really is good bar-b-que."

Jayson had a big smile and was trying not to laugh.

"What?" Shantelle inquired.

Jayson shook his head but continued to smile and started laughing silently to himself.

"What?" Shantelle pressed. "Why are you looking at me like that?"

Jayson still did not answer. He could not stop laughing to himself.

"What? What is so funny?" Shantelle insisted.

"You."

"What did I do?"

"You just try too hard. I'm fine. I'm a little cranky, but I'm fine. I really don't need cheering up, but thanks for trying."

"If you don't need cheering up, why did you snap on me?" Shantelle challenged.

"I did not snap on you," Jayson denied.

"You were yelling at me," Shantelle reminded him.

"I didn't mean to yell at you. I'm just going stir crazy around here. I'm used to a lot of travel and a lot of work. I'll try to do better from here on out, promise," Jayson vowed.

"It's okay. You just need to find something to fill the time. I'll try to be more understanding when you're antsy. You are overdue for a vacation, you know."

"If I am overdue for a vacation, so are you," Jayson pointed out.

"I know I am, but this isn't the way I preferred to take it."

"This isn't the way I wanted to take one either," Jayson agreed, "but here we are."

"Yep, if it helps, you're not alone. I think I'm starting to lose it too," Shantelle added.

"Have you checked into nursing classed yet?"

"No, not yet, but I'm going to."

"Okay, but you will, right? That will give you something to do, and I'll be going back to work in a couple weeks," Jayson planned.

Next Thursday Jayson was on cloud nine. "Good morning, it's a beautiful day with only six days to go," he greeted Shantelle.

"You're in a good mood."

"Why shouldn't I be? I can see the end of the tunnel, and there is a light at the other end. My side isn't bleeding anymore. It feels great. I will work again."

"You will? Was there ever a question?" Shantelle wondered.

"There for a while I wasn't sure," Jayson admitted. "How could you be so sure? It was a bad gash, and it bled out for so long."

"I know you better than that. I've seen you take on impossible odds and come out on top. I knew that you would come out on top this time too. I never had any doubt. I guess I know you better than you knew yourself this time."

"Thanks. Next time don't keep so quiet. Let me in on what you know I'm capable of," Jayson suggested.

Chapter Eighteen

Jayson stayed on cloud nine all day Thursday and all day Friday. Shantelle headed for bed by ten Friday night. Jayson who was still wide awake went to the kitchen to find a snack.

Shantelle walked into her bedroom and went to the chest of drawers to pull out her pajamas. She laid the pajamas on the bed when she heard a very faint noise from the bathroom. She walked to the doorway and called out in a flirtatious manor, "Jayson, come to bed."

"Huh?" Jayson called back.

Shantelle walked out of the bedroom slowly and quietly. She walked cautiously listening the whole way to the kitchen. When she got there, she took both Jayson's hands in her own and pulled him as close as skin. She leaned cheek to cheek and whispered, "There is someone in my bathroom."

"Okay, stay close to me, and do what I say," Jayson instructed. He held her hand and walked back to the bedroom with Shantelle. "Why don't you get ready for bed, and I'll be right there?"

Jayson walked into the bathroom. Everything was quiet. Everything was still. Jayson opened the door to the toilet. A scrappy, skinny man, who was covered in dirt from head to toe, hit Jayson. Jayson stumbled back only a step. He hit the intruder in the face with his elbow, and with one hit the intruder fell down unconscious. "Shantelle, call the police," Jayson called from the bathroom.

It did not take the police long to arrive, but it took an outstandingly long time before they left. Shantelle took a seat on the couch in the living room while the police looked around. She must have answered at least a hundred questions. Many of them were duplicated.

Finally the last two policemen left. Jayson sat down on the couch next to Shantelle and asked, "You okay?"

"Yeah, I'm fine. Who was he?"

"He was just a petty thief. His pockets were full of jewelry."

"Hah, the joke's on him. It's all fake."

Jayson laughed and took a deep breath.

"Being married to you is scary," Shantelle said out of nowhere.

"Wow," Jayson reacted with shock. He had not seen that one coming. Surely she didn't blame him for some two bit criminal breaking in to try and rob them.

"First, there's a strange, unexpected visitor at two in the morning. Then there is an intruder in the bathroom. What comes next?" Shantelle continued.

"I don't know. I never know," Jayson admitted, "but you handled it very well."

"He was hiding in the bathroom. He obviously wasn't coming after me. I had a small window of opportunity to get help."

"Impressive. Do I dare ask how you know all that?"

"The same way I knew to go to the girl's restroom and wait for Hawk's all clear," Shantelle answered. "Hawk knew my parents. I met him at their funeral. He takes my safety very seriously. When I started working for him, he drilled my head full of safety precautions and how to handle different situations."

"That's good to know. So, maybe being married to me isn't as scary after all," Jayson pushed.

"No, it's still scary. I don't care how prepared you are; it is still terrifying. I don't know how you willingly go out time after time and put yourself in those situations. I really don't understand why you're so anxious to get back to work."

"Okay then, being married to me is scary and terri-fying. That's exactly what every husband wants to hear. Thanks."

Shantelle looked over at Jayson. Tears were welled up in her eyes. She was trying hard not to start crying. He had been teasing her, but obviously she didn't get that.

"I'm sorry," she apologized. "I'm not trying to hurt your feelings. I never meant that as a personal attack. I was just stating a fact. It is scary. I'm scared."

"You're not okay."

"I'm not okay, and I'm not tired anymore," Shantelle admitted.

"That's alright. That's reasonable. It's a normal re-action, but it's all over now. Hawk has trained you well, and nothing is going to happen to you as long as I have anything to say about it. Come here." Jayson pulled Shantelle into his arms. He wrapped his arms around her and held her tight. He held her tight right there for hours until she finally fell to sleep. After she went to sleep Jayson loosened his grip and went to sleep himself.

Jayson woke up not long before Shantelle. Shantelle opened her eyes and lifted her head off Jayson's shoulder. She looked around groggily. "How ya' feel?" Jayson asked.

"Stupid," Shantelle answered honestly.

"You shouldn't. There is noting stupid about the way you handled things last night or the way you reacted," Jayson encouraged.

"Yeah, well, thanks," Shantelle said unconfidently. She stood up and started for her bedroom.

"Why don't I get the feeling you believe me?" Jayson called after her.

Shantelle did not answer. That was the last time they spoke about what happened. Shantelle avoided such a conversation at all costs. She certainly never brought it up herself, and she would go to the extreme of walking out on Jayson if he brought it up.

Elizabeth Lee Sorrell

Chapter Nineteen

On Wednesday Jayson did indeed receive good news at his doctor's visit. He was given the go ahead to go back to work. He was so anxious to get back that he stopped by the office on his way home to pick up an assignment.

"You're kidding. You already got your next assignment. You didn't waste any time," Shantelle reacted.

"No, I've wasted enough time already. I'm through wasting time. I talked to Hawk while I was there. He asked about you. I think he really misses you."

"Oh really? What gave that away?" Shantelle replied sarcastically. "How did the office look?"

"It didn't look that bad. The shredder is covered over, but there aren't as many files this time. I think he's getting the hang of it. I would put the shredding off till last if I were him too."

"There are still files sitting out though?"

"Yeah, but there's not half as many as other times we've walked into a mess."

"I don't know if that's a good thing or a bad."

"Of course it's good. Hawk has found a way to juggle a little filing into his schedule."

"I hope that's all it is," Shantelle mumbled.

"What else could it be?"

"I don't know," Shantelle admitted, but that did not put her mind at ease. Shantelle had a very bad feeling about the lack of filing to be done when the shredding was still piled up. The shredding is just as important. Hawk knows that. If he had found some extra time, why would he do one without the other. He would not. He would shred at least as much as he could get to. He would not just leave it to fall into the wrong hands if he could help it. Something was definitely off.

"Then stop worrying," Jayson suggested. "I'm heading out tomorrow morning. I've got an early flight. Are you going to be alright here? I'm sure I could make arrangements for someone to stay with you, or I could find you somewhere else to stay."

"Don't be ridiculous. That would realistically defeat the whole purpose for my moving in with you. If I'm going to stay somewhere else every time you're out of town, we might as well have kept my house. No, I'll be fine. I am fine. I wake up everyday a little stronger and a little braver. I was shook up immediately following everything that happened; that's all. It takes a little time to adjust to new things, especially for someone with a severe type A personality. I'm sure you agree I am a type A personality."

"Oh, no doubt. You are a classic example. You like everything in order all the way from your schedule down to your sock drawer. You can't stand any disorder. You are controlling. You want to fix everything including people who don't want to be fixed," Jayson described.

"Okay, okay, I get the idea," Shantelle interrupted. "The point is I'm fine. Go do your job. Have fun, and be careful."

"Awe, and to think, all these years I thought you didn't care," Jayson taunted.

"Yeah, yeah, keep that to yourself. I have a reputation to up hold," Shantelle played along.

Jayson was walking out the door the next morning when Shantelle woke up. "You going?" she asked.

"Yeah, I'm going. Are you sure you're okay?"

"I'm fine. Go on. Get out of here," Shantelle said frustratedly.

Jayson left Thursday morning. He returned Monday afternoon. Shantelle was in her recliner watching TV when Jayson walked in. "That didn't take too long," she commented.

"Nope," Jayson answered as he started to strip. He stripped all the way to his bedroom leaving a trail behind him. First his right shoe came off in the doorway. A step later his left shoe came off. His shirt made it halfway across the living room. The belt landed in his recliner. His pants fell in the hallway. One sock dropped in his bedroom doorway. The other sock made it almost to his bed.

Shantelle rolled her eyes and began following the trail picking it up as she went. She piled the dirty clothes up in Jayson's doorway while she hung his belt up in the closet.

Jayson made it to bed with his boxers and his undershirt still in tact. Shantelle had washed his sheets and covers while he was gone and made his bed. Jayson was sprawled out on top of the covers. Shantelle pulled the covers down and back over Jayson. Then she took the clothes down to the basement. How did this man ever get along by himself?

Jayson was already up when Shantelle got up Tuesday. He was in the kitchen when she went in to get breakfast. "Did everything go okay?" Shantelle asked with concern.

"Yeah, why?"

"Well, you weren't gone very long, and you were exhausted when you got back."

"Yeah, you're telling me," Jayson replied. "I don't even remember half the drive home from the airport. I didn't get much sleep while I was gone."

"How much is not much?"

"None," Jayson admitted, "but I'm rested now. Do you have plans today, or are you up for helping me with my report?"

"Yeah, sounds great. We can go after breakfast," Shantelle answered quickly. The excitement could be heard in her voice.

"You are anxious to get back to the office," Jayson pointed out.

"I am not," Shantelle denied. She sounded like a school girl in her denial.

"You are too. So, which is it that you miss so much, the work or Hawk?"

"Both," Shantelle admitted. "I'm curious to see what kind of shape the office is in. I feel sorry for Hawk trying to pull this through on his own. Plus I miss him. After fourteen years you tend to get attached to people."

"Yeah, I bet," Jayson agreed understandingly and let it go.

Elizabeth Lee Sorrell

Chapter Twenty

The office was not in as bad a shape as Shantelle imagined. The trash can was only nearly half full. The files were stacked neatly on top of the file cabinets. The stack to be shredded, however, was unbelievable.

"Why is there so much more to be shredded than there is to be filed?" Shantelle wondered aloud.

"Hawk's been filing, but he hasn't started shredding," Jayson answered nonchalantly. He was apparently not bothered by anything he saw. "Let's go ahead and do the report before someone else shows up."

Shantelle sat down and booted up the computer. "Hold up. I'm going to need a minute," Shantelle exasperated. "I hate other people coming in and using my computer. They're field agents not computer techs. They come in and mess with my computer, and then I have to come in and trouble shoot."

"No problem. Take your time," Jayson replied. He walked over to the shredder and started working while Shantelle fooled with the computer. It took longer than anticipated.

It took Shantelle a grand total of forty-five minutes to get the computer running correctly again. "Okay, I'm ready," she called Jayson back.

Jayson took a seat in front of the desk and said, "Someone must have messed the computer up pretty bad."

"You have no idea. Tell me about your assignment."

"You weren't here when I picked up the assignment. Do you need to know where it was and who it was?"

"No, I've got all that. Start with when you got there."

"Okay, the guy was easy to find. I spotted him as soon as I stepped off the plane. Get this. He was working airport security. That's a comforting thought, isn't it? A known terrorist managed to get a job in security at a major airport. Anyway, it was a major airport, and it was overcrowded. I couldn't take him out at the airport, so I tailed him. I figured I would follow him home, kill him at home that night, and be on my way home the next day. I was expecting a real short assignment. You should never assume things are going to be easy. That guy must have worked as much as you used to. When he finally left the airport, he did some running around, ran a few errands, and went right back to the airport. I waited at the airport and kept an eye on him. He did his sleeping at work when he was supposed to be watching monitors. Here's the scary part, he wasn't the only one. They were all asleep.

"This guy was left wide open. He had full reign of the airport, and no one would have asked questions since he was security. Sorry, I just have problem with that. These guys should be screened better before they are given a job at an airport, especially a security job at an airport.

"So, I'm still watching him. I'm jet lagged and I haven't had any sleep. He leaves the airport and meets a woman at a restaurant. They leave together and go to where I can only assume was her place. I remember the slash to my side, and I decided not to rush it this time. When he leaves her he goes back to the airport. By this point, I'm getting tired of the run around, not to mention I need sleep. Finally when he leaves the airport this time, he goes home. I snuck in, used a silencer, and shot the guy. Then I went back to the airport and caught the next flight home thinking I could get some sleep on the plane. Wrong. There was flight turbulence the whole way. I didn't get any sleep. That's why I was so exhausted when I got back. I had not gotten any sleep since I left. I was so tired, I could barely function. I don't know how I was functioning by the time I got home."

"You weren't functioning well by the time you got home," Shantelle added. "You looked like a walking zombie. You started stripping as soon as you walked through the door, and you stripped your way straight to bed."

"I'm sorry. That was very inappropriate."

"No, it's okay. You kept on your shorts and T-shirt. Really, it was fine. I wasn't offended. I followed behind you picking up. I had to. It would have made me nuts to leave it there in the floor," Shantelle explained.

"Thank you for cleaning my mess, and thank you for being so understanding. But, that was not okay. It was inappropriate, and I apologize," Jayson insisted.

"It's not that big a deal. Why are you so worried about it?"

"I'm not worried about it per say, but that's not the way I was raised. I was raised to be more respectful than that toward women."

"Oh-ho, this is coming from the admitted player," Shantelle accused.

"I don't think that the exact word used was player. I think it was something more like ladies man, but this is different."

"How is that different?"

"Being a gentleman and what women willingly give up have nothing to do with each other."

"Oh really? So, a gentleman fools around with women carelessly?" Shantelle pressed.

"Carelessly?" Jayson mumbled. "No, I was very respectful to every woman I fooled around with!"

"Oh, okay, I get it. It was a respectful one night stand, and you dumped them with respect the next morning," Shantelle shot back.

"Yes… no… I mean I did… Can we talk about this later? This is not an appropriate location for this conversation."

"Sure."

Jayson did not waste any time getting away from that conversation. He got up and took off for the shredder. He started shredding and never looked back.

Shantelle started filing. It did not take long to get everything filed away. Shantelle glanced over at Jayson. He had only put a dent in the papers to be shredded, but something did not sit well with Shantelle about the files she had put away. She went to the computer and pulled up a list of current and recent case files. The list included when it was issued, if and when it had been reported complete, and who worked it. "Hawk hasn't been filing," Shantelle said.

"What are you talking about over there?" Jayson asked still with a huffy attitude from before.

"Hawk hasn't been filing anything; there just hasn't been much to file."

"So what! What does that mean?"

"It means less is getting done. The amount of files are a direct reflection of the work load being carried out. The less there is to be filed, the less work has been done," Shantelle explained.

"What are you messing with over there?"

"There is less work being done because you are one of only five agents to do it. When I left Hawk was juggling twenty agents," Shantelle continued.

"What did you think was going to happen? People were not going to put up with the new rules for long. Get out of that. Come over here, and help me shred. We can get out of here sooner," Jayson suggested.

Shantelle shut down the computer and went to help Jayson shred. They did not talk for a long time. Finally, Shantelle broke the silence. She was speaking more so to herself. "I wonder how Hawk is holding up. I should check on him before we leave."

"He hasn't come out of his office yet. He must be staying pretty busy," Jayson commented.

Shantelle did not say a word. She did not appear to even hear Jayson. They finished the shredding, and Shantelle used the intercom to call Hawk's office. "Hawk, are you in there?"

"Shantelle?" Hawk responded.

"Yes, sir, can I come in?"

"Of course, come on."

Shantelle walked into the office, and Jayson slipped in close behind. Hawk looked awful. He looked like he had not shaved in at least a week. His clothes were wrinkled and hanging. He had lost a lot of weight. There were dark circles beneath his eyes. "How are you hanging in there?" Shantelle asked softly.

"They're killing me," Hawk admitted. "I've got almost nothing left, and I still can't find the hitch."

"The what?" Jayson inquired.

"You might as well know now," Hawk relented. "I believe that we are being sabotaged by the very board set forth to run this organization, but their plan is flawless; I can't find anything."

"Yeah, I know what you mean. I got the feeling that something was off when I went over the books, but I couldn't put my finger on it. Why didn't you say something? I could have helped before it got to this point," Jayson said.

Hawk looked accusingly at Shantelle. "I noticed something was up when there wasn't much to be filed. We know that there are only five agents left," Shantelle owned up to.

"I didn't want to say anything before because I was being cautious. I didn't know who I could trust and who

I couldn't, but Shantelle seems to trust you; that's good enough for me," Hawk replied.

"Is there anything I could help you go over?" Jayson asked.

"I've been over everything again and again. There's nothing here. There's not much left here to save anyhow. I can't see any way out. I started this department from nothing, and no matter what I do from this point on, that's exactly what will be left, nothing," Hawk sighed. "All I can do is try getting as much done as possible before we go down. That's why I've been trying to pass out the hardest cases we have. Have you picked up your next assignment yet?"

"No, sir." Jayson found it sort of odd that Hawk did not want any help going over anything. Two eyes are better than one. There may always be something that you simply overlooked no matter how many times you went over it, but Jayson could also understand why Hawk wanted him to continue working cases. Hawk was right; there was not much left here to save.

"Good, good, I've come across a very curious case. It seems we've had it for quite some time. It has apparently been hidden away incredibly well. It's one of the hardest cases we've ever had here, maybe the hardest. I prefer that you take it," Hawk said.

"Of course," Jayson answered quickly although from the excitement of the challenge or the eagerness to help he'll never know.

"I think I know which case you're talking about," Shantelle interrupted.

"I think you do too," Hawk said disappointedly. "Why was it hidden like that?"

"I had good reason for hiding that file. It's impossible. It's a suicide mission, sir, that can't be completed. The target, he's good; he can't be beat."

"No one is unbeatable, Shantelle. All humans are flawed. Eventually he will make a mistake," Hawk corrected.

"You don't know until you try, and I'm going to try," Jayson announced firmly with no room for discussion.

"You don't have to do this," Shantelle combated.

"I know that. I'm volunteering," Jayson replied.

"Please, don't do this," Shantelle pleaded.

Hawk pulled the assignment up on the computer and started it printing out.

"You can't do this. Please, don't do this," Shantelle continued to plead.

Hawk handed the assignment to Jayson. Shantelle jerked the papers out of Jayson's hands. "No! He's good. This is a suicide mission. You don't have to go... Please, don't go... Jayson, please, don't go," she begged.

Jayson took the papers back from Shantelle. "What is your problem?" he asked.

163

"Please, don't go," Shantelle responded in a soft whisper.

Jayson shook his head. He held the paper up and looked at Hawk. "Thanks, Hawk. Let me know if you think of anything I can do to help."

Jayson turned and walked out without looking back at Shantelle. Shantelle followed him out silently with her head hung low.

Chapter Twenty-One

On the way home Jayson decided to stop for
lunch. He did not ask Shantelle if she was hungry or
what she would like. He did not ask her anything. He
did not speak to her at all, but Shantelle did not
speak to him either.

Shantelle sat across from Jayson at the restaurant.
Jayson looked agitated. Shantelle looked scared and
upset. Still no one had anything to say. They ate in total
silence.

After the meal, the waitress went to run Jayson's
card. "How long are you going to look at me like that?"
Jayson demanded.

"Please, don't go," Shantelle responded.

"Is that all you have to say?"

"Please, don't go."

"I don't want to talk about this here. Just don't say
anything," Jayson told her.

Shantelle did not say anything else for a long time. They got home without another word. Shantelle followed Jayson back to his bedroom. Jayson got out a duffle bag and dropped it on the bed. Shantelle sat down on the bed next to the bag as Jayson packed.

Shantelle looked more upset than ever. She almost looked like she was fighting back tears. Jayson shook his head. "I can't believe you. You've never reacted like this to an assignment. I've never seen you react like this to anything. What is your problem?" he asked. He was still irritated, and it was coming through in his voice.

"Please, don't go."

"Is that all you can say? I am getting so tired of hearing that. What is going on?"

"Please, don't go."

"Okay, fine, obviously you don't want to discuss it like an adult. Don't. We won't discuss it at all. How is that?" Jayson shot back just tired of hearing the same pointless phrase repeated over and over and nothing else.

"Please, don't go."

"You are driving me crazy with that. Either tell me what's wrong or hush… I think I left my knife in the kitchen where I was sharpening it the other day. It's in a flat white box. Can you go get it for me?"

Shantelle left out of the bedroom and came back

with the white box clung tightly to her chest. Jayson reached for the box, but Shantelle was not letting go. "Please, don't go," she whimpered.

Jayson put his hands on Shantelle's shoulders. He rubbed her arms firmly. "Look. I know you're upset, but I don't know why. I don't know what to tell you if you can't tell me what's wrong. Listen. I've been doing this for a long time. I know what I'm doing. I understand that this guy is good. I'll be extra cautious… You have my word that I'll be extra cautious." Jayson reached for the box again.

"Please, don't go," Shantelle whispered.

Jayson forcefully took the box. She was really getting on his nerves. "Shantelle, I can't talk to you when you're like this. You're acting like a child, a stubborn child."

Shantelle did not say anything else. She silently watched Jayson finish packing. He packed a couple outfits, but mostly he packed weapons of various sorts. Jayson had his way of getting around airport security. It was never easy, but it could be done. It was considerably harder since nine-eleven, but it was still possible for someone who knew what they were doing. Jayson had explained it to Shantelle before. It had something to do with the bag and x-ray machines. If all else failed he could always take a private plane from a private airport. Shantelle had made arrangements for many agents on private planes over the years.

The next morning Jayson was up early to catch a plane. Shantelle was up just as early. "Please, don't go," she pleaded again.

"Tell me why. Give me one reasonable argument why I shouldn't go, and I will stop to talk about it calmly and rationally," Jayson offered.

"Please, don't go." She wanted to say something else, anything else. She wanted to tell him what was going on, but she couldn't find the words. They were lost somewhere in the fear and confusion that was controlling her.

"I've had enough. You sound like a broken record," Jayson said and left. Shantelle stood at the door and watched Jayson leave.

As soon as Jayson was out of sight, Shantelle turned and ran back into the house after her cell. She called Jayson.

"What?" Jayson answered harshly.

"Be careful."

"I promise," Jayson agreed.

It had been about three weeks since Jayson left. Actually it had been three weeks, two days, and forty-five minutes give or take a few minutes, but who was counting? Shantelle sat on the couch starring at a blank TV screen. She did not hear the door unlock or the doorknob start to turn.

Jayson walked in. He looked mad to put it mildly. Shantelle leapt up and ran over to Jayson. She wrapped her arms around him and exclaimed, "Oh thank heavens you're home!"

Jayson did not return the hug. He did not look happy. He did not look relieved to be home. He looked like a man on a mission. He appeared upset and looking for answers. "Why didn't you tell me?" Jayson demanded.

Shantelle let go of Jayson and backed away. "What?" she reacted with false confusion and innocents.

"Why didn't you tell me?" Jayson repeated.

"What are you talking about?" Shantelle asked as she started to walk away.

"Why didn't you tell me you knew him?"

"Him who?" Shantelle asked casually as she continued to walk away.

"Stop. Do not walk away from me. You know exactly who I'm talking about. Why didn't you tell me you knew the target?"

Now Shantelle had made it to the kitchen. Jayson followed her into the kitchen. "We've met before," Shantelle said as she took a bottled water from the refrigerator.

"No, Shantelle!" Jayson reacted inching closer to Shantelle. "You did more than meet him. You knew this guy, well. You're not willing to die for an acquaintance. This guy was willing to die for you."

"What?" Shantelle interrupted.

Jayson continued on as if he had not heard Shantelle. "Jealousy is a powerful emotion. I could have been killed. I know the risks in this job. If I had been killed because this guy was better or because I made a mistake, that was a risk I was willing to take, but I had no idea what I was walking into. Tell me now. How did you know the target?"

Shantelle pushed past Jayson. "His parent's were spies. We grew up together, somewhat. We both moved around a lot with our parents, so we grew up together as much as any two spy's kids could. We knew each other better than we knew anyone else. He was my first real boyfriend and my first real kiss."

"Why didn't you tell me?" Jayson demanded.

Shantelle paced around the kitchen with her eyes fixated on the floor. "I didn't think it was important."

"You dated this guy. I'm married to you now, and you didn't think that was important?"

"We were kids. We haven't talked in years," Shantelle tried to explain.

"But you hid the assignment, obviously trying to protect him, and you begged me not to go," Jayson reminded her accusingly.

"It wasn't like that."

"No? How was it?"

"All he ever wanted to do was be a spy. He started training himself at ten years old. His parents were proud that he wanted to follow in their footsteps. They encouraged him. They helped him, and they spared no expense. By the time he was old enough to apply, he was the best, and I'm not exaggerating. I saw him in action with my own two eyes. You're good, but he was better. I've never seen anyone as good as him. He has always been a bit of a rebel. Somehow over the years he just turned. It wasn't sudden; it was a slow process. I watched it happen, and I still don't know how it happened. He's good, and he's merciless. I didn't hide the assignment to protect him. I hid the assignment to protect our men. He would have killed them. He could have killed you. I begged you not to go because you could have been killed."

Her voice was shaky but not in a way that denoted a lie. She was having trouble getting the words out. It must have been hard for her to admit, and maybe the memories were painful as well. Just the same, Jayson had heard all he could stand to listen to.

"Alright, fine. I believe you. It was a stupid, stupid thing to do, but I believe you. I'm going to get a shower. Just… I don't care," Jayson said and walked out.

Jayson took a shower, got dressed, and snuck quietly through the house. It was starting to get dark outside. The TV was still off. Shantelle sat curled up in her recliner. Jayson reached for the front door. "Where are you going?" Shantelle jumped up.

Jayson took a deep breath and sighed. "I'm going to do my report. I'm ready to get this over with."

"You're not taking me with you?"

"I don't think so," Jayson answered. "I think it will be better for both of us if you stay here this time."

"I want to go. I want to know what happened. I need to know what happened, please."

"Well… okay, but you teach me how to do the reports. You show me everything you do… That way if it gets to be too much, I can finish it myself," Jayson relented.

"Thank you!" Shantelle exclaimed and followed him out.

At the office the night guards had already come on. All the lights were off except for a crack of light coming from Hawk's office. "Does he ever go home?" Jayson asked rhetorically.

"I don't think so," Shantelle mumbled to herself.

Shantelle booted up the computer. Jayson pulled a chair up next to Shantelle's. Shantelle showed Jayson how to pull up the correct program and how to get set up. "That last part we did can be done before or after, but I always do it before. That way when you get through typing up the report, you hit save, it saves and automatically shuts down the program."

Shantelle put the key board in her lap and turned to face Jayson eye to eye. "Are you sure you want to do this?" Jayson asked. Shantelle nodded. "You don't have to do this," Jayson said.

"Yes, I do. I've been really shook up since Hawk asked you to go. I need to know what happened."

"Are you sure?" Jayson asked. Shantelle nodded again. "Okay," Jayson started. "I got there, and I searched for six days. I found nothing, absolutely nothing. I couldn't even find proof that the guy had ever been there. Finally after a full week I catch up to him. He started leaving behind just enough evidence so that I knew he had been there. It was enough so that I knew I was always one step behind him. He was playing with me. It was a well planned game of cat and mouse, and I was the mouse.

"This went on for about three days, plenty of time for him to find out anything he wanted to know about me. Each location would have more evidence left behind than the last. It was like he was dumbing down the clues. He was basically making fun of me. Next he started leaving me pictures. They were pictures of me. I still haven't been able to make a visual on this guy, and he's been staking me out. He was better than me, and he wanted to make sure I knew it. He started leaving information on me and traces of various types of weapons, heavy duty weapons.

"Now I still haven't seen this guy. He knows exactly who I am and how to find me. He knows everything about me, and I am seriously out armed. I was a sitting duck. By this point I know that I'm already dead. Shantelle, shouldn't you be typing?" Jayson asked.

Shantelle was staring at Jayson in sort of a daze. She had quit typing several sentences ago. "Oh sorry," she suddenly snapped back. She caught up in no time, and Jayson continued.

"I never found him; he confronted me. He sent me down a deserted alley hunting for him. He was waiting for me. I was scared. I'd be stupid not to be. It must have been obvious because he called me out on it. He told me to breathe. He said he wasn't going to kill me because you meant too much to him.

"I told him that if he didn't kill me, I would kill him. He didn't care. He talked about you a lot. He said he knew you would end up with a spy. He was very hung up on you. I pulled my gun, but he still didn't care. He let me kill him. He just stood there and let me do it. He hated me. He didn't try to hide that, but he let me kill him anyway," Jayson remembered.

Shantelle continued to stare at Jayson deep in thought. The report was finished, but she had not hit save yet. She stared at Jayson. She started shaking her head. "No," she mumbled. Tears were beginning to well up in her eyes. "Oh, no," she breathed. Shantelle tossed the keyboard back on the desk. She jumped to her feet and ran down the hall. She turned into the women's restroom and disappeared from sight.

Jayson hit save. The report automatically closed, and he chased after Shantelle. He cracked the restroom door and called, "Shantelle." The light was off. Jayson opened the door and flipped on the light. Shantelle was sitting on the counter. She had her knees tucked tightly into her chin. Her arms were wrapped around her legs, and she was crying uncontrollably.

Jayson walked over to Shantelle. "I knew this was a bad idea. I should have never agreed to let you do this. Are you ok?"

"It's not the report. It's me. I'm terrible," Shantelle sobbed.

"What? That's crazy. Why would you say that?"

"It's true. I'm a terrible person," Shantelle insisted.

"Why?"

"I knew when you left that one of you would die. I was so scared that it would be you. The longer you were gone, the more I was sure you were dead. When you walked back in that door I was relieved. I loved him, but I am relieved. I'm relieved that he is dead. How can I be relieved that someone I loved is dead? What kind of person does that make me? I'm glad he's dead," Shantelle cried.

"Oh," Jayson said sympathetically. "Come here. You're not a terrible person." Jayson pulled Shantelle toward the edge of the counter. He slid her off the counter and into his arms. "You're not a terrible person. You're human. You're not relieved that he's dead. You're relieved that I'm not dead. To be honest, I'm relieved that you're relieved. I wasn't sure there for a while." He leaned down and kissed her.

Jayson smiled, and Shantelle smiled back. It was the first time he had kissed her the marriage ceremony aside. It was the first time he had ever really kissed her. He wiped the tears away from her face and kissed her again.

Suddenly Jayson pulled back. "Shantelle, that's it!"

"What?"

"Foster, he's the key. How much dirt can you pull up on Foster for me?"

"How much do you want? I've got unbelievable clearance."

"Are you ready to pull an all nighter?" Jayson asked. "I need as much on Foster as you can find."

"What is this about?"

"I think I might have found the hitch that Hawk has been looking for."

Chapter Twenty-Two

Shantelle went back to the computer and went right to work. Jayson sat down next to her. "Why are we investigating Foster?" Shantelle asked. "He's never said more than two words at a time."

"Exactly, he's quiet, too quiet. Why take a job on the board if he has nothing to say? Am I supposed to believe that he doesn't have an opinion? He never opened his mouth. He had nothing to say about everything going on. He lets Perkins do all the talking. He goes along with everything Perkins suggests. It could be that Foster is Perkins's lackey, but usually they're going to be the strong silent type. There is nothing strong about Foster.

"Try this scenario on for size. What if Foster's the head? He could be feeding Perkins instructions ahead of time so that he appears the follower. It's a perfect plan. Who would suspect the follower? Everyone hates

Perkins because on the surface he appears responsible. That makes Perkins the perfect distraction. We were all focused on the wrong guy," Jayson played out.

"Oh, that's interesting. Listen to this," Shantelle interrupted. "Foster applied for a job with the FBI at nineteen. At twenty-one he applied with the secret service, and at twenty-five he put in an application with the CIA. Each department turned him down. Apparently he didn't have what it took."

"That could make revenge the motive," Jayson chimed in.

"There's more. Don't underestimate. My clearance level would scare you. I can get you notes on all of the interviews. Which one would you like to start with?"

"FBI was his first choice? Try that one."

"Looks like it was a short interview. The interviewer was turned off from the get go. Listen to this: He walked in distracted. He's not observant. That's all the interviewer wrote."

"Try the CIA next since we branch from them," Jayson suggested.

"It starts out about the same. He can't answer simple questions about his surroundings. He offers information on small insignificant points, but he misses the obvious. He's smart, but he lacks a sense of toughness both mentally and physically. It is the opinion of this interviewer that he would be a liability and unable to withstand all that is involved."

"He definitely could have a chip on his shoulder."

"Oh boy... Hawk was the interviewer," Shantelle added.

At that very moment Hawk walked slowly out of his office. He was dragging himself along. He looked rough and half asleep. "What are you two doing here?" he questioned.

"We came up to do a report," Jayson answered.

"It's the middle of the night," Hawk pointed out.

"I wanted to get it over with. There were a couple surprises on this assignment that I'd just as soon put behind me."

"Shantelle, why do you look like you've been crying? Did he hurt you?" Hawk accused.

"No, of course not. It was silly. I'm going to be fine. I just need time to process... Hawk, why did you put Foster on the board?" Shantelle asked.

"He's smart. Did Foster do something to hurt you?" Hawk responded.

"You interviewed him when he applied for a job with the CIA," Jayson said.

"Yeah, what does that have to do with anything?" Hawk asked.

"Are you aware that he had already applied with both the FBI and the secret service?" Jayson questioned.

"No, I wasn't," Hawk stuttered in surprise.

"You didn't hire him," Jayson said.

"No, I didn't. He was smart enough, but he never could have handled the pressures that came with this job. When I started searching for board members, I thought of him," Hawk recalled.

"How smart is he?" Jayson questioned.

"Very smart. Why?" Hawk answered.

"Is he smart enough to take down an entire organization, an organization he has a grudge against run by the man who crushed his last attempt at his dream?" Jayson inquired.

"Sure, sure, he's smart enough to plan it out, but he could never pull it off," Hawk said.

"For someone so smart he hasn't had much to add," Jayson said.

"I've been very disappointed. I didn't ask him onto the board to take up space," Hawk admitted.

"So, why does someone so smart not have anything to say? If he's so smart, why does he follow Perkins as if he is incapable of having a competent thought of his own?" Jayson asked. "We've all been so focused in on Perkins that we haven't paid Foster any attention. Should we? How much do you really know about

Perkins? Is it possible that Perkins could be a mere puppet carrying out Foster's plans?"

"It is entirely possible. Perkins has never shown extraordinary leadership skills before. He's been successful, but that is mainly because of where he came from. He comes from a wealthy family, successful parents. He's had everything laid out for him, and he's worked that to his advantage. I was shocked to say the least when he took such a leadership role on the board. I did bring him onboard to take up space. He was basically a pretty face and a name to appease the political aspect," Hawk described.

"Jayson," Shantelle called. "Perkins has been arrested for narcotic possession. He was picked up six hours ago. His parents froze all assets, and they're refusing to post bail. The evidence against him is indisputable. He's not getting out of this one."

"Where's Foster?" Jayson asked.

Shantelle shook her head. "I have nothing on Foster for three days. He hasn't used a credit card. He hasn't used his debit card. He has his cell turned off. He's done nothing I can trace."

"If Shantelle can't trace him, no one can," Hawk added.

"I'm going to run out to his house," Jayson said.

"I'm going with you," Hawk offered.

"No, I'll go alone," Jayson denied. "You are in no shape for that."

"Jayson, in today's technology run world, if he can completely stay off the radar for three days, he's either real good or he's dead. Be careful," Shantelle warned.

"I'm just going to check things out. Keep digging. See what you can find. I'll be back." Jayson kissed Shantelle quickly and rushed to the elevator.

"I've searched everything over and over. I thought I had looked at this from every angle. How did ya'll figure that out?" Hawk asked Shantelle.

"I don't know. It was all Jayson. He asked me to look up everything I could find on Foster. Jayson is good, but he thinks he's invincible sometimes," Shantelle replied.

"Is that what the upset face is about?"

"Yeah, sort of."

"Does this have anything to do with that hidden assignment?"

"Yes," Shantelle answered honestly.

"Start from the beginning," Hawk instructed.

Shantelle proceeded to walk Hawk through the long chain of events spanning decades. The unnerving tale and digging for anything interesting in Foster's past kept both Shantelle and Hawk's time occupied while Jayson was gone.

Chapter Twenty-Three

Jayson parked his car a couple blocks away and walked the extra two blocks to Foster's house. The house was dark. Foster's car was out front. Newspapers were overflowing the mailbox. Jayson pulled his gun as a precaution and started sneaking through the yard. The grass was overgrown. It had obviously been ignored, untended for whatever reason.

Jayson slowly made his way around the house. He cautiously peered into each window. The house was spotless. There were no dishes in the sink. The bed was made. There was not a throw pillow out of place. There was no basement area. The house was deserted. Jayson broke into the house. He had not investigated in years. Working assassinations, all the investigative work had already been done. Jayson knew that he was a little rusty, but he was not picking up on anything. There was nothing to prove that anyone had ever lived there.

The carpet was not worn. All the furniture appeared to be in perfect condition. Dust had built up on the furniture. There were no fingerprints anywhere in the dust. The bed had no sheets, only a comforter and pillows. The closet was empty. The dresser drawers were empty. There were no towels or wash cloths in the bathroom. The kitchen had no dishes, no glasses, no pots, and no pans. The fridge and stove were neither one plugged in. From the outside looking in the house was nice, but if you look deeper, you realize that the house was not livable.

Jayson left the house and started back for his car. He called Shantelle. "Hey, no one is living in this house. What else have you found?"

"He has a brother in this area. The last time his cell phone was used, he was less than a block from his brother's apartment. The address is one-o-one Cherry Street, apartment two-B," Shantelle supplied.

"Great, I'm headed there now. Did anyone know Foster had a brother?"

"No, he's a half-brother. He's an older brother. His dad was in high school and never married the mother. His brother is a local PD. He's being investigated by IA."

"What about the dad?"

"The dad's dead. He was a U.S. senator. He was assassinated fifteen years ago. The case was never solved.

Hey, Jayson… could Perkins have been paid off with drugs that Foster's brother got a hold of? It shouldn't be too hard for an underhanded cop to get his hands on some drugs."

"That is entirely possible at this point."

"Oh, listen to this," Shantelle interrupted. "It was a big scandal when Foster's dad died. Apparently neither brother knew anything about the other. They met for the first time at a memorial service, a very volatile first encounter. All the follow-up stories claim that after a rocky start the two brothers became friends."

"Then why didn't we know anything about a brother?" Jayson pressed.

"I don't know. It's not on any of his files. There is no mention of any family. As far as the media is concerned there has been no public contact between the two since the last of the follow-up interviews were completed, and that's all I have to go on right now. We just missed it," Shantelle admitted.

"Okay, there's definitely something up with this guy. What do we have on Perkins?"

"I've been focused on Foster."

"See if you can find a way to tie the two. I'll check in later."

"Okay, be careful," Shantelle warned.

Unlike Foster's house, the brother's apartment was a mess. Dishes were piled up. Clothes were piled up.

Elizabeth Lee Sorrell

The carpet was stained. The furniture was falling apart. The bathroom had a strong urine smell. It was a one bedroom apartment with one bed. It was on the first floor. No one appeared to be home, and Jayson got the feeling that no one had been home for quite a while.

Jayson was leaving when his cell started ringing. "Yeah?" he answered.

"Jayson, Foster's brother was the arresting officer in Perkins's case. Perkins has been celled with two known hit men. Perkins knew both brothers and possibly their father. We have a newspaper clipping from the memorial service with a picture of Perkins in the middle with his arms around both brothers," Shantelle reported.

"We need something more substantial. Keep digging. There's no one here at the apartment. It has definitely been lived in, but I don't think that anyone has been here in a while. I'm going to take a look at Perkins's place while I'm out."

"Perkins's place is still a crime scene. Keep your guard up."

"He was busted at his home?"

"Yeah."

"Was there a warrant?"

"Yeah, but I can't find a reason for suspicion."

"Alright, keep digging. Follow any lead you find, and Shantelle, be careful. I've got a bad feeling about this whole thing," Jayson warned.

"I'm in a locked building that is federally guarded. You be careful."

"I'm being careful. You do the same, and if something goes wrong, I don't want you going to the bathroom. Get out of there."

"Okay, I will," Shantelle agreed. "What do you think is going on?"

"I don't know, but something's got me leery," Jayson admitted.

Perkins's place was large and harder to secure. Getting in and out was easy. Jayson went in through the basement. The basement looked like a playboy bachelor pad. Jayson noticed one life sized pin up that had been framed.

Upstairs the house had been trashed. It was very much deliberate. Someone had been looking for something. Even vent covers had been taken down in the search. No stone had been left unturned. Whatever the intruder had been looking for, if they did not find it then it was not there.

Jayson went back down to the basement curious why it had not been searched. The framed pin-up continued to pop out at Jayson. It was the only pin-up that had been framed. There were several pin-ups of the same girl all around the room, but this was the only one framed.

Jayson took the pin-up down and looked at the back of the frame. It had not been easy to frame, and whoever framed it did a sloppy job. Jayson turned the frame back around. He used his elbow to shatter the glass. He carefully took out the broken glass and pulled out the pin-up. Behind the pin-up were a picture and several papers. In the picture were four men at a college graduation. The four men were Perkins, Foster, Hawk, and someone Jayson did not recognize. The fourth man looked curiously like Foster. Although Jayson had not yet seen a picture of Foster's brother, he was positive that the fourth man was Foster's brother.

Jayson called Shantelle as he rushed back to his car. "Shantelle, get out of there," he instructed.

"But, Jayson, I found something. I've got a connection between Foster and Perkins."

"It doesn't matter. Get out," Jayson insisted.

Shantelle apparently never heard him. She continued talking right over Jayson without ever missing a beat. "They went to the same college the same years. In fact, they were roommates. They shared an apartment. Their names are together on the lease. They had two other roommates not listed on the lease. I'm pulling it up now… Oh!… Jayson…"

"Shantelle, get out of there," Jayson instructed, but before another word could be uttered the connection was lost. Jayson sped back to the office as fast as he could push the car.

Chapter Twenty-Four

Hawk was in his office. He had left the door open for a change, and he was eavesdropping on Shantelle. She was on the phone. She was talking to Jayson again, and she was excited. Hawk walked to the doorway to hear better. Shantelle had found the apartment lease from college that Foster and Perkins signed. Jayson could not get a word in edgewise. Hawk could not hear from the receiver what Jayson was trying to say, but he sounded frantic.

"Oh!… Jayson." Shantelle found the connection that put Hawk, Perkins, Foster, and Foster's brother in the same college apartment. They all four lived together for nearly six years. Hawk crept up behind Shantelle and hung up the phone.

"Black never could leave well enough alone. I never meant for you to get caught up in this. I love you like you were my own daughter. I let you go to keep you out of this. Sure, it's nice that Black is taking care of you, but I would have made certain that you were always provided for. Why did he not keep you out of this? He shouldn't have kept bringing you back. I was glad to see you; I won't deny that, but you should not have been here. He should have kept his nose out of it. Where is he, Shantelle?" Hawk asked.

"Why? I thought this place was your baby," Shantelle reacted.

"It is. This is the grand plan. I built this baby up. We all have roles in bringing it down so that no one can pinpoint the blame. Do you have any idea how much money there is to be made here?"

"But I thought what we were doing here was important," Shantelle stammered.

"It most definitely was. The work done here was very important while it lasted. The rise and fall, however, was purely a business deal. Don't look so disappointed. The work itself is still extremely important, and it will continue to get done. Every agent who worked here will get another job with another branch, another department. The assignments won't disappear; they'll follow the men and women who carry them out. They also will be passed on to another branch, another department," Hawk explained.

"What about Perkins's arrest? Was that a part of the grand plan?"

"That was unforeseen. He started using a few years back. He became a liability."

"His arrest was a set up," Shantelle commented with little need to question.

"Very good, Shantelle. You could have easily been an agent yourself."

"I don't have what it takes. Like Foster, I don't have a sense of toughness. Was not hiring him part of your grand plan?"

"No, I was honest in my report. He's smart, but he's not field agent material."

"What will you do now?" Shantelle wondered.

"I will return to my old job a richer man."

"What about Foster and his brother?"

"Well, that is entirely up to them."

"Aren't you afraid that Foster might still be angry at you for not hiring him?" Shantelle challenged.

"Of course not, he understands. I had to do what was right for our country in that situation. It had nothing to do with friendship or business."

"Obviously not," Foster said stepping out of the shadows with a gun pointed at Hawk. "A friend would have hired me. Even a business partner would not have been so cold. You aren't any good at either. Where's my brother?"

"How should I know? I haven't seen Tommy in years. We all agreed that it would be better if we had as little contact as possible," Hawk responded.

"Don't give me that. He's gone, and his house has been trashed. It looks as bad as Perkins's. I know you know something. You took care of him the same way you took care of Perkins, didn't you?" Foster accused.

"I don't know what you're talking about."

"No? How about now?" Foster asked as he pointed the gun at Shantelle. "Do you still think I don't have what it takes? Is this tough enough for you? Tell me where my brother is, or she dies. If he is already dead, she dies. If he dies before I get him back, she dies."

"I know where your brother is," Jayson's voice came from the hall. He stepped cautiously out of the dark. His gun was up and aimed at Foster. "Let her go, and I'll tell you where he is."

"Tell me where he is first," Foster negotiated.

"That's not the way it works. Let her go, or you'll never see your brother again," Jayson warned.

"What is to keep you from killing me if I let her go?" Foster asked.

"Nothing," Jayson answered honestly. "All you have is my word. You have my word that if you let her go, I'll tell you where your brother is. You also have my word that if you don't let her go within the next two seconds, it will only take me one shot to kill you."

"Fine, go to him," Foster instructed Shantelle. "Tell me where my brother is," he instructed Jayson.

"Not until she is out safely."

Shantelle walked slowly to Jayson never taking her attention off Foster or Hawk.

"Shantelle, the keys are in my right pocket. I want you to reach in and get them," Jayson guided. Shantelle reached in and pulled them out. "Get on the elevator and go downstairs. The car is parked on the East side of the building. Get in, and get out of here."

"How will you leave?" Shantelle asked softly.

"That's not important right now."

"I'm not leaving without you."

"This is not up for debate. Get out of here now, Shantelle. That is a direct order. Go," Jayson ordered firmly.

Shantelle kissed Jayson's cheek while tears streaked down her own. She moved quickly to the elevator. As soon as she was out of sight, Foster asked again, "Where is my brother?"

"I snuck in the back of the building. I saw a man in the shadows back there who matched a picture I found of your brother," Jayson answered.

Foster pressed the elevator button. As he waited for the elevator to return, he turned back to Jayson who was still pointing a gun at him. "If I find out you're lying to me…"

"I told you what I saw," Jayson replied.

Shantelle ran all the way to the car. It was parked just where Jayson said it would be. Tears were streaming down her face. She was crying uncontrollably. She could barely see through all her tears, but she climbed into the car and pulled away from the building anyway. Shantelle looked down at the seat beside her. Through her tears she saw Jayson's cell. She picked it up and dialed the director of the CIA.

"This is Shantelle White. We have an agent under attack on the second floor of our building. The only way up is through the elevator. There's possibly three other men besides our agent. The agent negotiated my release, but he is still there and in danger. Be advised, Hawk is one of the attackers."

"I need two minutes to get my men there. I want you in my office ASAP, White, for questioning."

Foster stepped onto the elevator. The doors shut. Jayson moved his aim to Hawk. "The interviewers were right. He's not as observant as he should be. Put the gun on the floor," Jayson instructed.

Hawk reluctantly eased his gun from the back of his belt to the floor. "The back up too," Jayson added. Hawk took the gun strapped to the inside of his left ankle and placed it on the floor. "And the knife." Hawk reached in his pocket and pulled out a knife. He dropped the knife to the floor. "Now kick them away." Hawk did as he was told.

"How long do you think it will take Foster to realize that his brother did not commit suicide?" Jayson asked.

"What do you want, Black?"

Jayson looked at Hawk with disgust. "Nothing you have to offer," he said.

The elevator returned on its own, out of the blue, but Jayson ignored it and kept his gun aimed at Hawk.

When the elevator opened and Jayson saw men with guns out of the corner of his eye, he swung his aim around to the men stepping off the elevator.

"CIA, drop your weapon," the men shouted.

Hawk lunged for the bottom drawer of Shantelle's desk. He pulled out a gun and fired at Jayson. Jayson went down.

One CIA man took Jayson's gun. The others all turned to Hawk. There were six men in total from the CIA. Hawk laid the gun down on the desk and put his hands up in the air. Hawk was cuffed and drug out, and an ambulance was called for Jayson.

Chapter Twenty-Five

Shantelle went straight to the director's office. "I only have one question to start off," he said. "What is going on?"

Shantelle went through every event leading up to that night. She described in grave detail everything that had happened. She was careful not to leave anything out no matter how insignificant it might have seemed at the time.

"Director, I'm sorry to interrupt," a man said opening the office door. "Agent Black has been taken to the hospital."

"Jayson!" Shantelle gasped.

"Thank you, Lowe," the director replied. The man nodded and left. "You're free to go to the hospital," the director told Shantelle, "but I want to be able to get in touch with you if there is anything else. Can we get you on the cell you called from?"

Shantelle pulled the cell from her pocket. "It's Jayson's" she mumbled. She nodded and added, "You can get me on it."

"Thank you, Mrs. Black," the director said with a wink. "You're upset. Please, let one of my men drive you to the hospital. They can use their badges to get you straight back to your husband no questions asked."

"That would be wonderful. Thank you," Shantelle accepted.

The ride to the hospital took longer than she wanted as everything crept by in slow motion. Each breath was harder to drag in than the last. What had happened? Was Jayson ok?

When they got to the hospital her escorts had to run to keep up with her as she sprinted though the halls, yelling for directions as she went.

"Jayson!" Shantelle exclaimed and she ran to his side.

Jayson was lying in a hospital bed. Thankfully he was not hooked up to any monitors or IV's. "What happened? Are you ok?" Shantelle asked in frantic desperation.

"I'm fine. Calm down. I was shot in the shoulder. It didn't hit any bones. The bullet came out the other side. It tore through the muscle, but Dr. Hanson says I'm going to be just fine. I just need time for my shoulder to heal. Looks like I'm back on the DL."

"DL doesn't sound so bad when you take into account that you don't have a job to return to."

"Actually, I would like to correct that situation for both of you," the CIA director interrupted pushing his way into the room. "What Hawk started was not a bad idea. His intentions, however, were more questionable. I need someone I can trust running things. It won't be an easy fix after the number that Hawk pulled. I need someone who knows the program and can salvage it. I need you, Shantelle. You'll run the program, and your husband will have a job to go back to. What do you say?"

"You want me to take over in Hawk's position?" Shantelle asked in amazement.

"Can we get back to you?" Jayson interjected.

"Of course, I know this type of decision takes thought. I want you to take your time. Talk it over. I hope that you'll be confident in whatever decision you make. This is a vitally important position," the director agreed and excused himself.

"What did you send him away for?" Shantelle demanded from Jayson anxiously.

"I didn't send him away. He left on his own," Jayson pointed out.

"Jayson," Shantelle whined.

"You've never been a whiner; don't start now."

"Jayson, you knew what I meant. Why are you aggravating just for the sake of aggravating?"

"I'm not aggravating simply for the sake of aggravating. Why are you so eager to take the offer before you think it over? Is that what you want? What about nursing? I thought that was what you wanted. You've already started classes, haven't you?"

"I have actually started, but who said I had to quit? A lot of people are part-time students and still work a full-time job. Besides, nursing skills could prove to be invaluable. Do you have any idea how many agents come in beaten and broken?"

"Is it possible this time? I know a lot of people do it, but most people don't have a job this involved. If you take that job, you'll be putting in a lot of long hours, and when you're not at the office, you will always be on call," Jayson pointed out.

"Jayson, do you think I don't know that? I know what the job entails. I know the job better than anyone. I know better than you what I'm getting into, and I know I can do it," Shantelle insisted.

"I'm sure you can, but do you want to do it?"

"I do. I really do."

"Then call the director, and let him know the decision you made."

"Are you serious?" Shantelle asked excitedly.

"Yes, go call him."

Shantelle spun around on her toes to go put in a call to the director of the CIA.

"Shantelle," Jayson called softly, stopping her retreat, "I love you."

"I love you too," and she did. Marrying Jayson Black had been the best decision that Shantelle White had ever made.

Also Available from Elizabeth Lee Sorrell

Wrong Turn Fairy Tales

Gwynn worked hard to live up to her family's expectations putting away all childish things and even a few childhood friends. Now she is about to marry Addison, a very sensible, very rich businessman, but before she can say yes to his proposal, she finds herself falling through one fairy tale after another. Will she find her happily ever after with her very  own prince charming, or has her fairy tale taken a wrong turn?

Exclusively found from Barnes & Nobles for Nook Book.

More Than Instinct

Kat had a past best left forgotten. Jackson had a past he couldn't get over, but when circumstances throw them together in a dangerous game, they had to find a way to work together. What they would find was that, "This whole mess had bonded them in a way that could never be undone."

Available from your favorite bookstore.

The Clause Rebellion

You would think that being the daughter of Santa would be a dream come true, but you would be wrong. Wynter Clause is miserable. She wants to get away, so she goes to the one place where she knows no one will look for her, the South Pole. Unfortunately, everyone in the South Pole hates the Clause's. Hiding her true identity seems the only way to survive. Will Wynter be found  out? Will the South Pole people accept her? Will Wynter ever step up to the duties that she left behind in the North Pole?

Available from your favorite bookstore.

Coming Soon from Elizabeth Lee Sorrell
More from The Clause Rebellion Series coming fall 2017!

Also from our Author... Children's Books

Sugar Sugar On a Stick

Who doesn't love a good lollipop? Is it possible to love them too much? What would you do with the power to magically create lollipops? One little girl finds out, but will the cost be worth the sugary prize?

Doofy the Hippo?

Doofy does not want to be a hippo any longer. Does he change or accept himself? Maybe both. Enjoy this book as you discover how Doofy learns to be happy with himself in a world of beautiful differences.

The Faceless Nutcracker

When a beautiful golden, faceless nutcracker shows up in Christmas Town, everyone forgets that true beauty is far more than skin deep. The faceless nutcracker creates a diversion by messing up Santa's naughty and nice list. He and the naughty children of the world go on the attack spreading hate rather than love.

Can anyone stop them?

The Life of a Firework

Come with us as we follow the life of a firework. What are his biggest hopes and dreams? Will those hopes and dreams come true?

About the Author

Elizabeth Lee Sorrell is an Alabama native. A gifted teacher, she has worked with babies and preschoolers, from her teens all the way to today. She is a teacher in the Federal Head Start program. She has her Associate's Degree in Early Childhood Development, her Bachelor's in Early Childhood Education and Elementary Education, and her Master's in Early Childhood Education.

When not teaching, or leading as the Nursery Coordinator of her church, she is with her family and dear friends, probably reading or writing a book. She loves to spend time with her nieces. Elizabeth is a Christian. She cheers for the Auburn Tigers, and the Atlanta Braves. As a big baseball fan, she has, more than once, written stories in the world of MLB, and watches as many games as she is able. One day you may just have the pleasure of reading one of those stories.

She enjoys pairing up with Sandra JS Coleman for her covers, layouts, and illustrations. Sandra, Elizabeth's sister, is a graphic designer and an illustrator.

Learn more at www.ElizabethLeeSorrell.com, and don't forget to follow on Facebook as well.

Colophon

Cover design, etching on cover, and interior layout designed by Sandra JS Coleman (where applicable Adobe Software was used).

The typefaces used on the cover and interior are Garamond Premier Pro and Alana for the book title, Baskerville for the body, chapter titles, and other text, and Anglecia Pro for the Yarbrough House Publishing Logo.

Robert Slimbach was inspired by Garamond's metal punches and type designs in 1988 to create Garamond Premier Pro, by the. Laura Worthington designed Alana. She is a typeface designer from Washington State. Baskerville is a longstanding typeface. Not Old Style or Modern, it is a transition typeface designed by John Baskerville in 1757.

The book was printed in the United States of America, on 50lb white paper, perfect bound, with a gloss cover.

CPSIA information can be obtained
at www.ICGtesting.com
Printed in the USA
BVOW06s2306210617
487524BV00009B/59/P